When The Cookie Crumbles

A novel by

Carlos Harleaux

WHEN THE COOKIE CRUMBLES

Copyright ©2019 by Carlos Harleaux.

Published by 7th Sign Publishing

(www.PeauxeticExpressions.com)

ISBN 978-0-578-45880-9

Book Cover Design by Bruce August, Jr.

Photography by Richard Mudd (Mudd Productions)

Table of Contents

Chapter 1

Ken rubbed his hands down the arch of Cookie's back, before resting them comfortably on her behind. He felt like he was floating. They both moved in unison with a feverish, unspoken rhythm. With each kiss, another fire was ignited inside of him. "Damn baby, I'm not going to be able to last too much longer if you keep moving it like that," he whispered in Cookie's ear.

"Oh, is that right? Well, in that case maybe I should just keep it up and make you explode. Would you like that? Would that make you smile?" Cookie replied, barely able to breathe and maintain her composure.

"I'm holding out. I want you to get there first. But you're not making it easy for me," he grunted, flipping Cookie on her back as he moved slowly in and out of her. He scooped his arms around her waist as she thrusted her pelvis harder and faster. There was no way he could keep up like this.

He pushed her hips down on the bed and took control of their movements. They both climaxed together, not even minutes later. Ken fell limp on top of Cookie and didn't even recall falling asleep. She really drained every part of him. He wasn't complaining though. He loved it.

Ken felt like an eternity had passed when he woke up. He laid behind Cooke on his side, with his arm wrapped around her mid-section. He felt her move, as the sun started peering through the curtain. Wait. The bedroom didn't look familiar. Why was Cookie's hair longer? Why did it have blonde streaks? This could not be.

. . .

"Ahhh. Damn. You sure know how to make a woman weak in the knees," Melissa said, with a devious smile on her face. Her back was still turned to him, but she squeezed his arm tightly around her. She fantasized about Ken being inside of her for a long time. She knew she was wrong for sleeping with Cookie's husband, but she just couldn't help herself. Ken was irresistibly sexy and she knew he wanted her too. He was a faithful type of man; a rarity. So, she knew she had to take matters into her own hands if she wanted a piece of him.

"Amazing. Well, I must say that my knees aren't exactly strong right now either. I'm still tingling," Ken responded. Something wasn't right though. His head was pounding hard near his left temple. He felt like a steeping teapot, just ready to blow at any second. Ken stumbled hard as he got up, almost falling back on the bed.

"Hey, watch it now. I didn't know I had that kind of effect on you. Everything ok? Here, drink this," Melissa replied.

"What is it?" Ken asked suspiciously.

"Just a little water, enhanced with electrolytes. You should be feeling back to normal in no time. Maybe you're just a little dehydrated. I know you need to leave soon, but I'll be right back. Don't go anywhere," shed ordered.

"I'll be right here," Ken said. He peeped around the corner to make sure Melissa was out of the line of sight to the bedroom. Ken had just made the biggest mistake of his life. He was surely attracted to Melissa. However, he never intended on cheating on Cookie with her. He felt a wave of nausea come over him suddenly. That's when it hit him.

* * *

Ken couldn't remember much of anything after last night. He only remembered bits and pieces. He left his iPod at Melissa's office and she kept it in her purse. He told Cookie he was going to meet her to get it. The plan wasn't to meet Melissa at her house. She gave him a drink last night too. A mimosa. He knew he shouldn't have taken that drink from her. Everything else after that was a massive blur. He looked over at her purse, sitting on the side of the bed.

He could hear her shuffling some dishes around in the kitchen, so he had time. He stuck his hand inside her purse. First, he felt a gun. Then, a few lipstick tubes. Ah, that's it. He ran his fingers across a pill bottle and took it out of her purse. He leaned over the other side of the bed and placed the bottle in his coat pocket, right before Melissa walked back in the room.

"Oooh, you are making it so difficult for me," Melissa whined, as Ken stood up from the bed, putting his underwear and pants back on.

"I can't do this again. Seriously, this was the first and last time," he said, putting his shirt on and carefully picking up his jacket. He knew it wouldn't be easy sticking to his word. Melissa wasn't necessarily better than Cookie in bed. No woman he had ever been with was better than her. Melissa was a close second, though. Plus, the thrill of releasing the long-standing tension between the two of them was exhilarating.

"I know. Karma is on its way to us, I'm sure. Can a girl at least bask in her glorious moment though?" she smiled. "Here, this is a little concoction I make whenever I have those woozy feelings. I promise, it's not another mimosa this time".

* * *

"Hmmm, ok, I'll try it I guess," Ken smirked, nervously accepting the glass. His memory served him correct. He did have a mimosa when he got to her house last night. He just still couldn't remember exactly what happened after that. Ken tasted the drink, which was orange juice mixed with something spicy. It burned a little on the way down.

"Ginger?" Ken asked, peering up at her suspiciously over the glass.

"Yep. I know, it tastes a little strange but it's a great pick me up. Trust me. I guess it's a good thing our last session is coming up. I wouldn't want to make this anymore complicated for both of us than it has to be," Melissa said, with genuine concern.

"True, we can't let this happen again. Well, I won't let it happen again," Ken replied. He sounded more like he was trying to convince himself rather than Melissa.

"I understand completely. Oh, well please don't forget your iPod. It's right there on the counter. After all, that is what you came here for," Melissa smiled nervously.

"Oh, yeah. Right. Thanks Melissa. I'll see you at the session," Ken said, as he grabbed his iPod and walked toward the door.

"Ok, sounds good. Good bye, Ken," Melissa said, as she closed the door behind him. She slid down the inside of the door as tears began to stream down her face. The reality of what she had done set in. Her desires completely took over her. Cookie trusted her and they started to bond outside of the therapy sessions. This was not going to end well.

* * *

Meanwhile, Ken picked up his phone to dial Cookie. He quickly ended the call before it connected. He needed to wait until he got back home. Thank goodness she was out of town for work. There would have been absolutely no way he could explain coming home in the morning without letting her know of his whereabouts. Ken looked back through his text message history and saw that he did text Cookie to say goodnight shortly after 10:00 pm. Thankfully, she was hanging out with some of her coworkers and didn't text him back until a couple of hours later.

"Hello? Hey baby! The best part of waking up. Who needs Folgers, right?" Cookie smiled, still half asleep yet excited to hear from her husband.

"Look at you, making me blush. I just called to say good morning baby. How is the conference going so far?" Ken asked.

"Oh, it's great. I think I'm already starting to feel the struggle of getting up for two people though. Even though I haven't started to show much yet, I have a feeling this baby is not going to be a morning person. Maybe if I play my cards right, you can be the designated person to make sure he or she is out of bed on time. What do you think it will be?" Cookie asked, talking a mile a minute. Her pregnancy hormones were kicking in. She was never this talkative in the morning.

Ken's heart dropped to the pit of his stomach. What was he thinking? How could he have done something so reckless, especially while Cookie was pregnant? There was an uncomfortable silence over the phone before he responded to Cookie. "I'm so grateful to have you baby. I seriously don't know what I ever did to deserve you," he said, swallowing the huge lump forming in the back of his throat.

* * *

"Aw, well now you see how I feel about you. You're going to be such an excellent father," Cookie responded.

"Thank you, baby. You're going to be an outstanding mother too. You're already great at trying to boss me around," he laughed.

"Excuse me, sir?" Cookie laughed, caught off guard by his sarcastic comment.

"I'm just joking baby. I guess I better get going though and head into work. I'll be checking on you later today," Ken said.

"Ok, that sounds like a plan. I need to get a move on it myself and prepare for this meeting. Love you baby," Cookie replied.

"I love you too. Oh, my bet is it will be a girl," Ken said.

"Ah, well my bet is on a boy but time will tell," she giggled. "Bye baby".

Chapter 2

"Bill. Wake up baby. I made some pancakes for you, with the pecans. I know that's how you like them. Remember to lay off that bacon. These are some veggie meat patties. Tastes just like the real thing. I swear you won't know the difference. There's some scrambled eggs here too and some freshly squeezed orange juice," Lisa smiled, showing all of her beautiful teeth. Even in her older years, she still looked much younger than her age. She kept her appearance and health up well.

"You are amazing baby. This food smells phenomenal and it looks even better. I should be the one up cooking you breakfast. I don't know about those veggie patties though," he laughed, giving them a disapproving glare. His countenance quickly turned sour as he poured a glass of orange juice for Lisa first and then himself.

"Hey, I don't like that face. What's going on in that head of yours? Did I forget something with the meal? Are you feeling ok?" Lisa asked, with a serious look of concern on her face.

"Oh yeah I'm fine baby. Just truly grateful for you, that's all," Bill answered. Deep down, he knew that she knew he wasn't telling the truth. Lisa didn't want to make an awkward scene in front of the kids. She went along with his response, despite her taunting intuition.

"Candice, do me a favor and go grab your sister for breakfast. Make sure you both wash your hands first," she instructed. She waited until Candice walked away, before directing her attention back to Bill.

"I'm just fine baby. I didn't realize I was hungry before, but all this food has worked up an appetite. I love you," Bill said, kissing Lisa on the cheek. He was trying to give her reassurance that nothing was wrong with him. He wasn't totally convinced it was working.

"Ok, if you say so then. Where are the girls? This food is going to get cold. Candice! Chelsea! Time for breakfast!" Lisa yelled. Chelsea and Candice came marching in, with wide smiles and anticipation for the delicious meal. Bill led the family in prayer before they enjoyed the food.

"I take it that you girls really are enjoying your mother's food," Bill laughed. "Slow down there Chelsea. The plate will still be right there". She took her time with her next bite, before quickly going back to her rapid routine.

"Well, look who's talking Mr. You're not exactly eating slowly there yourself," Lisa smiled at Bill. Everyone finished the rest of their breakfast. Candice and Cookie were both still little girls and were a ball of energy. They couldn't wait to help clear the table so they could play outside together. Lisa made them promise to help her clean the kitchen first. She believed a woman should always know her way around a kitchen and keep a clean house, no matter how successful she may be.

Bill and Lisa could hear the girls screaming and chasing each other in the back yard. They both were the cutest little tomboys who didn't mind getting dirty. Candice and Chelsea could be prissy when they wanted to be, but they were also as athletic as many of the boys.

"Alright now, it's just us. Go ahead and tell me what's really on your mind. I know there's something going on in that head of yours. You can tell me. You know that, right?" Lisa pleaded.

Bill's eyes started welling up as he tried to hold back his tears. He just grabbed her hand and looked her in the eyes. He tried to muster up the words, but his vocal chords were paralyzed. "Yeah, I do know it. I do," was all he could manage to say.

"Bill, I know that look. You've been acting strange lately. Come on. Spill it! Are you sick? Did you lose your job? Are you.....wait? Please don't tell me, you cheated on me," Lisa replied.

Bill's stare may as well have pierced straight through Lisa's soul. He remained silent, which confirmed her greatest fear. "It was Janice. One night after the guys and I were hanging out after the basketball game. I had a little too much to drink. I made a bad decision. I'm so sorry baby. I hope you can forgive me," Bill said, with a cracked voice.

"Please. Don't do that," Lisa replied, with a stoic expression. "I love you Bill and we're going to fight through this; but I'm not your "baby" right now. Was I your "baby" then too? My mom was right. Every man really does cheat. I thought you were different," Lisa responded.

There was a painful, thick silence that floated in the room for what seemed like an eternity. "Mom! Can we have some juice?" Chelsea busted through the door.

"Um, yes baby. Go right ahead. It's in the refrigerator," Lisa said, wiping the corners of her eyes.

● ● ●

12

"Wait. I can get it myself?" Chelsea asked. She was surprised her mother was letting her have free reign with the refrigerator, something she hardly ever did.

"Too funny. Ah, you are right baby. If I leave you to it, you might get too much. Don't forget about your sister too. Let's get her some juice," Lisa smiled.

"Mommy. Is everything ok?" Chelsea asked, moving her gaze back and forth to her mom and dad. Even at five years old, her intuition was spot on. She may not have been able to pinpoint exactly what was wrong, but she knew something wasn't right.

"See! That just proves my point. I've only met your dad a couple times. No disrespect, but if he cheated then every man cheats!" Angie exclaimed, talking to Cookie over lunch. They decided to have lunch offsite during their work conference. Angie was a divorce' who always jumped at the chance to talk about how men were no good. She professed it so much to the point that Cookie suspected she may have become a lesbian.

"Well, thank you for giving me hope," Cookie laughed. "My dad was wrong. He really was, but my mom handled it with such grace. She did whatever she could to protect us from any harm. They both did. To this day, I don't think my dad knows that Chelsea and I know about it. Ken hasn't given me a reason to think he's cheating though. I can't watch him 24/7 and I don't even have the energy. If a man or anybody for that matter is going to cheat, there's nothing you can do to stop it. Cheating isn't a deal breaker as far as I'm concerned though," Cookie said, nonchalantly.

. . .

"I just can't be that girl. Take Bryce for instance. Now, I didn't catch him cheating, but my intuition Is always spot on. I'm telling you, Cookie. I could feel it in my bones. So, I had to let him go. Save yourself the heartache," Angie said.

"I get it. I'm all about the intuition and the gut instincts. Trust me. I've been down that road before. But shouldn't you leave some room to trust? Shouldn't there be some room for the other person to just eventually show their true colors?" Cookie asked, trying to talk some sense into her coworker.

"I suppose. But sometimes you need to take that litmus test into your hands and force them to show those colors. That's all I'm saying," Angie laughed.

"Girl, come on. Let's go. I don't even know how I always get roped into these debates with you," Cookie replied, laughing.

****

Meanwhile Melissa was just stepping out of the shower at home. Her first appointment was at 1:00 pm, so she had no major need to rush. She still couldn't believe how good it felt to release all the pinned up sexual frustration between her and Ken. Although she had to create the opportunity in an unconventional way, she had no regrets. She did wonder how this would impact her relationship with Cookie though. Nevertheless, she had to make sure her sexy secret stayed under wraps.

She turned on the TV and there was a talk show talking about men who had cheated on their wives. She quickly turned away, as she didn't want to have her sins completely thrown back in her face so quickly. Melissa thought about how awkward it would be the next time she saw Cookie. They were scheduled to meet for lunch next week. Dammit. She would just have to cross that bridge when she got there.

Melissa grabbed her purse, keys, phone and walked out of the door. She reached inside her purse before pulling out of her garage to grab a tube of lipstick. She found the lipstick but didn't feel the bottle of pills that were inside of her purse. Shit. Where did they go? They must have fallen out of her purse last night. Hopefully Ken didn't see them. She shook off the notion and told herself that Ken couldn't have been that smart. Most men hate digging in a woman's purse anyway. She was sure she would find the pills underneath her bed or somewhere in her bedroom when she got back home.

Melissa's first session of the day was one she was not looking forward to. Phil Princeton was an alcoholic and a sex addict. Something about him was particularly creepy though. She could never quite put her finger on it, but she often felt uneasy in the room alone with him.

She stopped by La Madeleine on her way into the office. She loved treating herself to their strawberries Romanoff on days that she needed an extra umph. She ordered a large serving, along with a small chicken Caesar salad. However, she already started it off well with a great night with Ken. She was still pleasantly sore from their erotic episode.

She settled into her office and looked at the clock. 12:30 pm. She had just enough time to eat her food in peace before Phil arrived. He was extremely prompt, so she expected him to arrive a couple of minutes early. Melissa was just taking the last Romanoff dipped bite of her strawberry, when she heard a knock on her

* * *

door. 12:56 pm. She was certain it was Phil. "Come in on," she said as she adjusted her blazer and took a seat on the plush, cream colored couch.

"Hello Melissa. How are you on this fine Tuesday morning?" Phil said, giving Melissa a timid gaze as he sat on the identically designed couch across from her.

"I'm doing quite well. You seem to be in an exceptionally great mood today. Tell me how you've been since our last appointment. Anything new? I know you had to cancel the last couple of sessions. Is everything ok?" Melissa asked. She was genuinely concerned, but also realized pulling information from Phil was an art. He hardly ever answered questions directly.

"New? There have been so many new things since then. Trust me. You wouldn't have the time for all of that in one session. That is unless you're open to continuing our session outside of these walls," he smirked deviously.

"That won't be necessary. Let's just make the best use of this session. Shall we?"

"Ok, well I must admit. I had a bit of a relapse during our last two sessions. I was in a bad place then. Really dark…you know? Alcohol likes to tell me it's my best friend. But I think we all know it's not. I felt sooooo good though. Just floating in it all. I had not a care in the world," Phil explained.

Melissa kept her composure while her insides were screaming at him to give her something that made sense. "I'd say that's cause for celebration. You recognize that alcohol in excess is not good for you. That's a great start. Do you realize how many people can't even admit what you just said? Go on. Tell me more. How do you feel now that you've come to this new sense of mental clarity?"

"Let's not get ahead of ourselves. Now that I think about it though, I should maybe give myself a round of applause this week. At least I can say I didn't overdo it with the alcohol. Yes. That was a sure win. But there are other things. Kinky. Painful. Secret things," Phil whispered.

"Ok, it's a safe space here. What kind of things are you talking about?" Melissa asked cautiously.

"Do you remember that old Prince song, "Pink Cashmere"? It goes like this, "I'm making you a coat of pink cashmere. You got to know how I feel about you. Got to always have you near". Whoo. That song is just like sex in a bottle. Anyway, I went to this little thrift shop last week and I found the perfect pink velvet jacket. It wasn't exactly cashmere, but you get the point. My goal was to hold on to it until I found the perfect woman to fit it. That must have been my lucky day. I found her. She was beautiful, with breasts just large enough that I knew she would barely be able to button up the jacket all the way to the neck," Phil said.

"This is quite the escapade. Yes, I do remember that Prince song. He's one of my favorite artists. How flattering of you to pick up this coat and give it to the woman you deemed worthy enough to wear it. I'm sure she was honored," Melissa responded.

"Oh, that's an understatement. I made her strip, put on the jacket and only button the top button. Just as I hoped, her breasts were too large for her to button it all the way down. We had the most intense sex ever. Have you ever had that kind of sex, Melissa?

* * *

That kind that makes your blood boil, your toes curl and the pit of your stomach turn back flips?" he asked.

"I think it's safe to say I'm no virgin, but this isn't about me. Go ahead. I want to hear the rest of your story," Melissa answered curtly.

"Ok, if you insist. I brought out my leather whip and tied her arms to the bed. I spanked her repeatedly until she screamed for more. I think I may have hit her a little too hard at some points, though. Her moans of pleasure turned into shrieks as I whipped her so hard she began to ooze blood. It tasted so divine. Mmmm.....bon appetite. Oh and when she climaxed, it was like the floodgates came rushing over me! She was grateful and I was excited to oblige her fantasy," Phil exhaled.

"Oh my. Well, what exactly did that experience provide for you in terms of our session today? What did you learn from it?"

"Don't you interrupt me! Did I say I was finished? Melissa, your breath has that sweet fragrance. Strawberries, with Romanoff specifically. Another hard day or just an indulgent treat? What keeps you up late at night? What makes your floodgates open? I know you. You're a nasty little closeted freak. I know you are," he tossed his head back and laughed.

Chapter 3

"Hey baby, do you ever think that maybe Ryan was right about this house?" Sheila asked, as she poured the waffle batter mix in the griddle. She really enjoyed cooking, but there was something special about cooking for her husband. She had never been married before, but she was elated to be with Sean forever. They had just arrived back into their new home. Everything happened so quickly. The wedding; their new house; the honeymoon. Everything was overwhelming, but in a good way.

"Hmmm. Why do you say that? I don't think there's anything wrong with the house. I thought this was what we both wanted," Sean replied in a perplexed tone.

"Don't get me wrong. I absolutely love the house. I couldn't have asked for a better home to live in. It's just the aura. Maybe there's more to that story that we don't know about. I mean, think about it. There's got to be a deeper reason why Ryan wanted us to stray away from this house. Something other than that lady flipping crazy on him at that Christmas party," she laughed.

"Well, I guess you do make a good point. I can't say I've noticed anything weird. I love the house. Most of all, I love that you're in it," he smiled, feeding her one of the strawberries on the cutting board, with some whipped cream.

"Look at you. You always know how to make me melt. If you don't mind grabbing some plates good sir, I will finish the eggs. Ooh! These shrimp and grits are amazing, if I do say so myself," she smirked, tasting a sample of her dish.

● ● ●

"I didn't marry you for your cooking, but I must say this is a nice perk. You can really throw down baby....in more ways than one," Sean smiled, grabbing her waist and kissing her on the forehead.

"Go on now, nasty. If we get something started, I'll burn this food. Do you mind pouring us some juice from the refrigerator? I guess you're right about the house too. I just feel like there's a presence in here sometimes. Almost like there's someone watching us. Does that make sense?" she asked.

"Wait a minute. Don't tell me we have a poltergeist situation in here. Do we need to call an exorcist?" Sean laughed.

"Baby, it may sound crazy. I'm serious though. The other night when we were watching TV, I felt like someone was walking outside of our bedroom door after you fell asleep. It was so creepy. I'm telling you," Sheila said in a serious tone.

"Why didn't you tell me that? That's not cool. Maybe you should reach out to Cookie to see if she has any more of that magic dust," he said.

"Hmph. I'm surprised you even remember me telling you about that. You may be on to something, though. I need to call her anyway. I'm so excited to be an auntie soon. That girl deserves all the happiness her feisty little heart can hold," Sheila responded. An unexpected wave of sadness suddenly came over her.

Sheila and Sean sat down at the table, said their grace and began to dig into the delicious breakfast that Sheila prepared. "Mmmmm, baby you really outdid yourself with the food. This is delicious. I love it," he smiled excitedly, not knowing which bite of food to take next.

* * *

"That makes my heart smile. Eat as much as you want. There's plenty. I'm so glad to hear that you like it," Sheila replied.

"Baby, did you leave the door to the garage open last night? Looks like it's cracked now," he said, walking over to shut the door.

"Sean, I know I shut that door all the way when I came in last night. Good thing the garage was down though. At least we would have heard if someone was trying to get in through there. I was tired though. Hell, I possibly could have left it open by accident. Planning the menu for that wedding reception has been a beast. Marcy and Aaron hardly agree on anything, let alone the food for their wedding. Honestly, I'm surprised they even get along well enough to be married," she ranted.

As soon as Sean closed the door, glass shattered inside the garage. "Whoa. What the hell was that?" Sean said. He opened the door quickly and turned on the light switch in the garage. Everything was still dark inside. He grabbed his cell phone and turned on the flashlight from it. He didn't see anything at first, until he turned the light up towards the ceiling.

"Everything ok baby?" Sheila asked, getting up from the table to look over Sean's shoulder.

"Hmmm. That's weird. Have you ever known a light bulb to blow out with the light switch off?" Sean asked.

"No. I've never seen that before. That bulb is completely shattered. I'll get the broom," Sheila said.

"Ok, just leave it right here. I'll sweep it up. I don't want you to get any of this glass on you. Good thing we have some extra bulbs. I'll sweep around the cars first and then back them out to change the light," Sean replied.

"Just be careful please. Come on, let's at least finish our food first. Then we can clean up the mess later," Sheila pleaded.

****

Bill went for a mid-morning walk, showered and prepared to run a few errands. He decided to go purchase a couple of pieces of salmon and a nice wine to have for dinner later that evening. Although he toned down his physical activity since Lisa died, he had to keep busy. He was able to cope with her death a little easier, without an idle mind.

He was very healthy for his age and still looked youthful. He attributed it to not taking life too seriously. However, when it came to Bill's family, everything turned into a serious matter. He was the epitome of the male provider and protector stereotype. Bill's persona made some people believe he was emotionless. Those close to him knew that he had a heart of gold beneath the façade.

Bill was not in denial that his days were lonely without Lisa. He handled this hardship like he did anything else in his life. He trudged forward the best way he knew how. Bill grabbed his keys, opened the garage and drove to the nearest Whole Foods. He made the mistake of going there hungry, which made him buy more than he intended. He only had a smoothie after his walk; hardly enough for a man of his stature.

He walked up to the shortest checkout line. "Bill?" he heard a familiar female voice calling him. He had a hunch as to who the

* * *

lady was. When he turned around, his guess was confirmed. She was probably the last person he expected to run into today.

"Well isn't this a nice surprise? Mrs. Caldwell, it's so great to see you. You look well. How are you doing?" Bill asked, mustering up more concern than he really possessed.

"Oh, you know, I'm making it. Some days are harder than others. But I'm making it. One day at a time. I guess we both are, right?" she answered, with a light sigh.

"Very true. Things just aren't quite the same with Lisa. I can imagine it's the same for you with Caldwell too though. I know I miss watching the games and arguing over who the best teams were," Bill smiled.

"Yeah, you know Caldwell. Lisa was a phenomenal woman. It was truly a pleasure just to know her. I don't mean to throw a wrench in your plans. I'm sure you have a lot to do. Um, but call me some time if you're just bored or maybe need someone to talk to," Cathy replied, with a coy smile.

"Oh yes, I will definitely do that. It was nice seeing you Cathy. You have a great rest of your day," Bill said, giving Cathy a gracious hug before getting in line to check out.

● ● ●

Chapter 4

Cookie stared at the ceiling in her hotel room. She had just gotten out of the shower and was lying on the bed in complete silence, rubbing her barely bulging belly. The hotel's robe was so plush and warm. She felt like she was enfolded in a layer of clouds. Her body felt completely relaxed, but she still wasn't able to fall asleep yet. So many thoughts were racing through her brain.

She enjoyed the quiet time alone, but she was also anxious to see Ken. Cookie never liked being away from him for too long. That yearning intensified after she found out she was pregnant. She sympathized for Ken, because she knew she must have been even more of a handful to deal with now.

The most frightening thing was her repeated, vivid visions of her sister. Although it had only been a few months since Chelsea's death, she still had difficulty thinking of her in past tense. There were times she wanted share exciting news about her pregnancy, fly her sister out for a girls' weekend or just simply check on her to see how her day was. All of that was impossible now.

Then there were times she could see Chelsea's face watching over her. Ken always liked to brush it off as her being a guardian angel over Cookie. The thought was flattering and preferred over what Cookie was witnessing. Chelsea never had an angelic look on her face in any of Cookie's visions. She looked tortured, angry and at times, evil.

Cookie would never quite get over feeling like she could have done more. She could have stayed at home in Chicago to help watch over her baby sister. She didn't have to move to Dallas. Chelsea really needed her, whether she liked to believe it or not.

* * *

Ironically, Cookie always admired her sister's strength. A piece of her even envied it.

Her phone rang and woke her up out of her daydream. She had a hunch that it may have been Sheila. She was right. "Hey girl. How is my happy newlywed doing?" Cookie smiled, propping herself up against the headboard of the bed.

"I am fabulous. How is my little niece doing in there? You know I can't wait to meet her," Sheila responded.

"Well, thank you. I'm doing just fine. I tell you. This baby has everybody forgetting about me and my feelings nowadays. Wait a minute. Niece? How are you so sure it will be a girl? We were going to just wait and be surprised, but we agreed it would probably be easier if we knew the sex earlier on. Funny thing is Ken swears it will be a girl too. I think it might be a boy though. Either way, I just want a happy, healthy, non-fussy baby. Do you know what I mean? Sheila? Are you still there?" Cookie asked.

"Oh yes, mam. I am right here," Sheila said.

"Well why were you so quiet then?" Cookie said.

"Cookie, I'm telling you this with the sincerest love I have in my heart for you. I can really understand Ken's position right now. I see what they mean about those pregnancy hormones. Lord, you are probably driving that man to drink!" Sheila laughed.

"I am not! You are just so wrong. So wrong. Girl, truth be told I probably am. I feel like I am all over the place lately. I feel like I'm always telling Ken to look over me," Cookie responded.

* * *

"Hey, there is nothing wrong with that. I'm just giving you a hard time. Use this to your advantage. Pregnant women can damn near rob a bank and be excused for it. I do have a rather strange question for you," Sheila asked.

"Ok cool. Go ahead, shoot. What's that?" Cookie answered, curious to see what her friend would ask.

"Well, do you remember that weird purple dust that old gypsy lady gave you at the fortune teller shop in New Orleans?" Sheila said.

"Yeah. How could I forget? What about it? Don't tell me something has got you spooked now. What's going on?" Cookie replied in a joking tone.

"Spooked is definitely the word. Cookie, it's this house. There's nothing wrong with Sean. I love him and he is one of the best things that has ever happened to me. There is something strange about this house though. We both had a shady feeling about it, but we just brushed it off. Just this morning, the light bulb in the garage shattered. Nothing even hit it. Sean thought I was exaggerating at first, but I think he even believes me now," Sheila continued.

"So, I'm guessing you want to put some of the dust in your house? Sheila, I don't know if that stuff even works. I was just caught up in the moment when we got it," Cookie answered.

"Well, how do you know? It could have held off some evil spirits you didn't know about. I'm willing to try it," Sheila responded.

"Has the feeling gotten stronger since you moved in? How strange did you feel about the house before you moved in?"

Cookie asked. She was fully invested in her friend's potentially haunted house now.

"It all started with our realtor, Ryan. He conveniently left out the fact that he was stabbed by his ex-wife at this house. I'll send you the article. Her name is Melissa something or other. His ass was probably cheating. I guess she just got fed up with it and stabbed him. Who knows? The aura in that house is weird," Sheila said.

"Wait a minute. I'm looking through this article now on my phone," Cookie said, reading the story and talking to Sheila through speaker phone. "This woman that stabbed him is the counselor that Ken and I have been seeing. It's a small world. I'm sure she had good reason, but I just can't believe she did that!"

"Believe it. She did it and he caught the brunt of it. I don't know Melissa, but I think I like her. She obviously doesn't take any shit from a man. My kinda girl," Sheila laughed.

"I'm just a little surprised she never shared this story with me. You have to meet her. She's so real and honest. She doesn't seem like a push over by any means. This is a bit extreme though," Cookie said.

"Well, no shit. I don't know too many people that will divulge that they have ever stabbed someone in the heat of passion," Sheila laughed.

Cookie laughed at her friend's frank rationalization of Melissa's actions. "Ok, I guess you do make a good point. She probably wouldn't have said, "Hi, I'm Melissa and I stabbed my ex-husband. Back to that dust...Ken would be thrilled that it's out of the house now. He never liked that I kept it anyway. I get back in town tomorrow. Let's meet for lunch this week. I'll bring it with me," Cookie said.

"Ok, nice. That sounds like a plan. Plus, it will give me a good excuse to see you," Sheila replied.

"Yeah it will be good to catch up. Love you girl. I'm going to try to get some rest, but I'll talk to you soon," Cookie said.

"Ok, get your rest. Have a good night. Love you too sis," Sheila said.

Cookie smiled as she hung up the phone. She may have lost her sister Chelsea, but Sheila was as close as a sister could get. They went through many highs and lows together. Somehow, they weathered every storm and always formed an even stronger bond because of it. Cookie attempted to close her eyes and get some sleep. However, her thoughts kept circling back to Melissa. She wondered what else Melissa may have been failing to mention about her life outside of work.

****

Meanwhile, Ken's best friend, Charles randomly called him at lunch. He and Charles were both so busy. Nonetheless, they had the kind of friendship that easily picked up right where they left off. His wife, Alicia, was a real gem too. She was funny, witty, down to earth and an attractive woman to boot. In many ways, she reminded Ken of Cookie.

"Well, look who I finally got ahold of," Charles joked when Ken answered the phone.

"Man, there you go. I know I've been MIA. Work and getting prepared for this new baby has been taking up all my time. Although I know that's no excuse man," Ken responded.

"It's ok man, believe me. I know how you feel. Ken is a father now. Man, I can't believe it. Cookie is a special woman. Alicia has been bugging me about us all getting together. She's on this kick about making the most out of life and cherishing the people you love. One of her close friends just found out she has breast cancer. You know how it is. She is paranoid about everything now. I agree with her though. We aren't getting any younger," Charles said.

"Wow, I hate to hear that. Let's do it. We have to get it on the calendar. How are the next couple of weeks looking for you all? I miss my little man Lance. He should be getting ready for little league football soon, right?" Ken asked. Ken didn't use the word friend loosely. He always kept his circle small and close. Charles was the same. So, it only seemed fitting that he would be the perfect person to be Lance's godfather.

"I know next week will be pretty tough, but the week after should be perfect. I'll wait until you talk to Cookie before I tell Alicia. I don't want her to get her hopes up. Yep, Lance is too excited. He gets his uniform next month. He's been marking his calendar, counting down the days. He's actually pretty good too. We are excited about it," Charles replied.

"Well, too bad we can't say he takes after his father," Ken snickered.

"You have jokes man. I don't remember you out on that field in high school either," Charles laughed.

• • •

"Hey, I knew my place and I stayed in it. I think we'll be able to work something out the week after next though. Cookie is out of town for work, but she'll be back tomorrow. I'll be sure to let her know. I'll confirm it by this weekend. You know you all haven't seen the house yet. Maybe you can come stay with us for a weekend," Ken suggested.

"That would be awesome. Lance would love that too. I told him that you and Cookie have a baby on the way. Man, you should have seen his reaction. You would swear that it was Alicia and I having another baby. He really looks up to you," Charles said.

"I'll be so glad to see him. Cookie and I were talking about all of you the other day. I know she is going to be so excited. I probably should get back to it man, but it was good catching up. We are overdue for a happy hour too. Believe it or not, I can still hang just as tough as I could when we were in our early 20s," Ken laughed.

"Oh yeah? Don't talk about it. Be about it. We will see about that then. We'll catch up. Don't forget. Talk to Cookie and let me know what she says," Charles said.

"Definitely will do. Looking forward to it," Ken replied.

"Me too. Talk to you later," Charles replied, before hanging up the phone.

Chapter 5

Angie waited for Cookie to come out of the restroom before they walked towards their gate for the flight. "Hey girl. Everything ok?" Angie asked, as Cookie walked out of the restroom.

"Oh yeah, I'm fine. Just a little pregnant woman bladder syndrome, I guess. I have to pee all the time now. Thank you for asking though," Cookie said.

"Well, I would say I know what you mean. I can only imagine. I admire you. I just think I'm too selfish to ever have kids. I told myself if it doesn't happen by the time I'm 40, I've just resolved I'll be ok without a baby. A little life waiting on you to feed it, clothe it, change it, entertain it. Whoo. I'm tired just thinking about it," Angie giggled.

"You always have a way to find the not so silver lining of any cloud, don't you? Girl, come on let's go. Ken will kill me if I end up missing this flight," Cookie laughed. She took a selfie of herself blowing him a kiss. She texted the picture to Ken with a message that read, "Your baby (and your baby ☺) is coming home! XOXO".

"Oh good, we still have about 10 minutes before it's time to board. Can I tell you something serious?" Angie asked.

"Of course. Sure, what's that? Goodness, I'm so out of breath. I haven't gained a lot of weight, but I am feeling every pound," Cookie exhaled.

"I'm proud of you. You are a kick ass superwoman at work. You have a wonderful husband that is quite the catch. Plus, you are about to start a family. I know I joke a lot about how no good men are. I think you really have something real with Ken though. That's what I want. You're blessed, girl. The pickings out here are like finding a needle in a haystack," Angie said, with a serious tone.

"Wow. I really appreciate that, Angie. You will find it, I'm sure. The funny thing is Ken came to me at a time when my mindset was like yours. I wasn't looking for a man. In fact, I really didn't want to be in a relationship. I was perfectly fine with casual dating and a night cap when I felt like it," Cookie stated bluntly.

"Mmm, look at you. I know that's right. I'm a firm believer that women should do to men what they have been doing to us for years. Take that control back," Angie chimed in excitably.

Cookie and Angie went on to talk about women switching the roles on men until it was time for them to board the flight. Cookie realized she misjudged Angie. She didn't see her as someone with much substance before their trip together. She knew Angie was great at her job. However, she didn't think there was much beneath the surface. Angie made the trip more relaxing and less hectic. She was a breath of fresh air that Cookie embraced.

Their seats were near each other, but Cookie wished they were seated together. She was quite exhausted from the trip and was looking forward to catching a nap on the plane. However, her heightened sense of awareness, due to her pregnancy, didn't allow her to get too comfortable with the idea of falling asleep. Thankfully, Angie was just one row in front of her, diagonally at the edge of the isle. Cookie sat in the window seat to avoid having anyone cross over her. She would have been perfectly fine if she had the entire row to herself. Just when she let out a sigh of relief, an elderly woman sat down next to her. Angie looked back and

* * *

locked eyes with Cookie, but quickly turned her head to avoid laughing. "Well, how are you doing young lady?" the woman asked.

"Oh I'm doing just fine. How about yourself?" Cookie really could care less about how the lady was doing. She just wanted a short nap on the flight. She didn't even have to sleep the entire way home. Dammit! Was that too much to ask? Just her luck that she got stuck with a motor mouth on the way home.

"Well, my knee sure is bothering me today. I had to have surgery on it a couple weeks ago. I was a bit frustrated about it because I thought a 50-year-old lady like myself should not have to have knee surgery. I'm active and I still have some youthful years ahead of me. My doctor said it's not that uncommon," the lady barely took a breath long enough for Cookie to respond.

"Oh no, I hate to hear that. Don't feel bad. You look way younger than 50 by the way. It must be all that physical activity you've been doing. You really look great," Cookie said. She nearly made herself throw up from the lies she was telling this lady. The woman easily looked 62. Cookie thought buttering her up would give her a nice self-esteem boost; maybe it would keep her quiet too. She was wrong.

"Well I appreciate that vote of confidence. You know what the trick is? Water, good sleep, no alcohol, no drugs and good sex. Contrary to popular belief, you shouldn't have too much of the latter. You don't want to put too many freeway miles on that car if you know what I mean. Just enough to keep that engine purring. Oh, look, a baby!" the woman said, stretching her hand towards Cookie's stomach to touch her barely noticeable baby bulge.

• • •

"Ah, please don't," Cookie said abruptly, moving the woman's hand away before she touched her stomach.

"Forgive me. Where are my manners? I should have just said congratulations and left it at that. Although I am impressed. You look quite young. That kind of superstition is usually reserved for older women in my generation. They believed it was heebie-jeebies trouble if a stranger touched their pregnant belly. Great danger. You know?" the woman said, playfully raising her hands in panic. "It's nice to see the younger generation holding on to some of those older ideals though. It's quite refreshing."

"There are a few of us out here that have some old-fashioned values, I guess. I really didn't mean any harm by it. It's just my first child and I'm probably a little overprotective," Cookie smiled.

"Baby, you don't owe me any apology. It's your prerogative. Do what you feel is best. Oh, and forgive me for being so rude. My name is Ruby Sneed. What's yours, my dear?" Ruby asked.

"My name is Candice. It's nice meeting you," Cookie replied. By this time, the stewardess was making the announcement for everyone to fasten their seatbelts and power down their electrical devices. She also went over standard safety rules and precautions; the part that no one really pays attention to.

Ruby pulled out a book from her purse and started thumbing through it. "This is when I get to catch up on all of my good books. I was visiting my sister here. You know how family is. I had a wonderful time, but I am ready to get back home. Everyone wants to tell you how you should live, how you should eat and who you should marry. Last I checked I was grown. Honey, three days was more than enough for me," Ruby ranted.

"Believe me, I know exactly what you mean. Family has a way of being that thorn in our side sometimes," Cookie replied, with her eyes glossing over. She fought tears thinking of her mother and her sister. Cookie would still psyche herself out sometimes and believe that they were just out of town. She wiped her eyes and quickly changed her thoughts. The last thing she wanted to do was start crying in front of Ruby and be interrogated about it.

Thankfully, Ruby was thoroughly into her book shortly after takeoff. Cookie could not have been more grateful. Now, she could get some rest on the flight. She was not able to shake her thoughts of her mother and Chelsea. They followed her into her dreams. This one felt more vivid than any of the other dreams she had. She was on a larger plane, but this time she was sitting in the middle of Chelsea and her mom.

The three of them were having a blast, laughing, catching up and telling stories. The strange part about it was there was no one else on the plane but the three of them. Suddenly, their laughter turned to terror. "Wait! Mom, Cookie do you see this?" Chelsea said, pointing outside the window. The clouds looked heavy and dark. The sky had a purple and red tint, as if it was bruised and bleeding.

"What is going on out there? This doesn't look safe. Goodness. We still have another three hours before we land," Cookie said, looking down at her watch. The plane suddenly jerked and flipped sideways, with its right wing straight up into the air. Cookie, Chelsea and her mom all started screaming. Cookie could feel her air supply being cut off. It was harder for her to breathe.

● ● ●

She tried to reach up to grab her face mask, but accidentally knocked it to the floor. They still didn't see anyone on the plane, not even the pilot. Cookie, Chelsea and her mom had to fend for themselves and do whatever they could to survive.

Chelsea was able to reach in the seat behind her for an extra face mask and pulled two more for Cookie and her mom. They held on to their seats as the plane flipped completely upside down and barely back right side up. They felt like they were on the wildest rollercoaster of their life. Cookie could feel her heart pounding in her throat.

Ruby shook Cookie hard and she woke up feeling bewildered. She looked outside and the sky had a burnt orange tint. The clouds were whizzing by and she could see something that looked like a tornado in the distance. "Everyone just stay calm. We are going to get through this. We just have come across some turbulence," the pilot said.

"Oh my God. I'm so scared. How long has this been going on?" Cookie asked Ruby. She felt the pit of her stomach go down to her feet. The front of the plane tilted towards the ground quickly, which propelled her forward in her seat.

"I'd say about 10 minutes ago. You've been sleeping for about an hour. Everything was smooth and then you could just feel the wind moving the plane. I'll be glad when we get through this. I've been on a few turbulent flights before, but this is by far the worst," Ruby responded.

"Cookie! Are you ok?" Angie asked, trying to stand up out of her seat so she could see Cookie's face. She had a frightening look and was clearly nervous for her and her friend's safety.

* * *

"I'm ok. Thanks Angie. This is scary. Shit!" Cookie said. This could not be the way her life was going to end. She started praying and clenched her eyes shut. Looking outside the window and at the other passengers only made her more nervous.

The plane took another deep nose dive, before the pilot was able to navigate it parallel to the ground again. Ruby clenched the seat pocket in front of her, with her head down towards her lap. "Not me too...Not me too...Not me too," she chanted over and over again. Cookie couldn't help but wonder why Ruby kept repeating those words. She thought it might be a good gesture to try to say some comforting words to her.

"Ruby, we're going to make it out of here just fine. You know that, right?" Cookie asked her, with a tinge of doubt in her voice. She was shocked at Ruby's response.

"No, we're not! This is the same way my brother died. In a plane crash! My God. How dare you serve me the same fate!" Ruby screamed.

"Wait, Ruby. I'm truly sorry to hear about your brother, but you must believe we will make it out of here alive. We are not going to crash and God didn't give you the same fate as your brother. I'm sure of it," Cookie smiled through her tears.

"Everyone, thank you for remaining calm. We are now exiting the turbulent zone. We will have to take a detour to ensure we have a smooth flight the rest of the way in. We apologize, but there will be about an hour delay from our designated arrival time.

* * *

Chapter 6

Ken checked his watch and waited about five minutes before sending Cookie another text message. "Hey baby, it's me. I'm here. It's 5:30 now. Just getting a little concerned," he texted. His heart was racing as he was waiting to hear back from Cookie. This would be his first time seeing her since he slept with Melissa. He couldn't believe that she would be having his child in four months. Pregnant. Dammit. He couldn't remember if he used a condom with Melissa. What if she was pregnant too? What if he caught an STD?

Another 10 minutes passed by. Ken was still anxious about Cookie, but it had only been about 30 minutes after all. He used the spare time to set up an appointment with his doctor next week to make sure everything was ok. He still had a challenging time grasping that his memories from that night were so vague. He only remembered coming to Melissa's house, talking for a bit and then waking up in her bed the next morning.

Then, he remembered the pills. He should have researched them before picking up Cookie. That had to be it. Those pills needed to be his alibi to get out of this unscathed. He wasn't sure Cookie would believe his story. Either way, he needed to tell her soon.

He leaned his head back in the seat, closed his eyes and exhaled deeply. Ken's phone sounded off two message alerts. He quickly picked it up; both messages were from Cookie. One was a selfie that she took on the plane. Her face looked slightly troubled. Maybe the flight was a little rough for her, but something didn't look right. Then he saw her second message that read, "I landed

* * *

safely babe! I have so much to tell you and I can't wait to see you ☺".

Hmph. If she only knew, he had so much to tell her too. Ken got out of his car and walked towards the terminal. He responded to her text, "So glad you made it in safely baby. I'll be waiting for you at the gate. I love you and can't wait to hear about everything 😊." His hands were sweating so much he could barely type the letters on the keypad.

Ken saw Angie first, then spotted Cookie walking right behind her. He saw another woman he never met before, walking by Cookie's side. She looked like she was talking a mile a minute. Cookie didn't seem too enthused by what she had to say. He saw her reply to the woman as if to excuse herself before she met eyes with him.

"Hey baby! Goodness, I am so glad to see you baby. Ugh. I love you so much," Cookie said, wrapping her arms around his neck and giving him a hard kiss on the lips. He was flattered by her excitement to see him, despite being taken a back a bit from it.

"I know she is happy to see you. We had a hell of a turbulent flight. I tell you, it was scary. We are all ok and most importantly, your baby is just fine," Angie said, patting Cookie on the back.

"Whoa. Wait. Turbulence? What happened on the flight?" Ken asked Cookie, with a staunch look of concern on his face.

"Well, thanks for spilling the beans before I could open the can Angie," Cookie laughed. "Yes, I was going to tell you babe. It was wild. I think it got to me more though because I woke up to it. It was during the middle of the flight. Oh, and Ruby, this is my husband, Ken."

"Alright, well I'm all ears to hear about this story. I may need to go have a word with the pilot. Nice to meet you Ruby," Ken replied.

"Yes, likewise. I know we all must get going and I am ready to take a hot bath and have a glass of wine. Today has been quite the ordeal. It was a pleasure meeting all of you. You have a wonderful evening," Ruby replied.

"Aw, you too Ruby. Pleasure meeting you as well. Be safe getting home," Cookie said.

"I sure will. Take care," Ruby responded.

"Yes. Have a good one," Angie said, as Ruby walked away. "Damn, I thought she would never be quiet. That flight had a way of putting some things in my life in perspective. But, geeesh. That woman was a nonstop chatterbox. Cookie, I'm sorry you had to sit next to her," Angie laughed.

They all started walking towards the baggage claim as Cookie explained the horrific story of their flight. She tried to play it down for Ken, but she could tell the thought of it really frazzled him. "Baby, the important thing is we made it here safely. I was really scared though, I can't lie. You know what the strangest thing about it all was though?" Cookie asked.

"What's that?" Ken asked.

"It was almost as if I had a premonition about it. That or either I was feeling it as it was happening in my sleep. I had this dream right before I woke up that my mom, Chelsea and I were on a plane by ourselves. No one else was there. We didn't even see the pilot. The same thing started happening in my dream. There was this crazy turbulence happening and the sky looked like it was bleeding. I tell you, these pregnancy hormones must be no joke," Cookie smiled, rubbing her stomach and looking up at Ken.

"You can't scare me like that. I love you baby," he said, kissing Cookie on the forehead. They had just made it to the baggage claim. Angie's suitcase rolled by quickly. She picked it up and gave her last hug to Cookie and Ken.

"Well, Cookie, this was definitely a great trip. I'm going to make sure that if I have to go to anymore work conferences, you have to come with," she laughed.

"Thank you, Angie. Same here. I really had a great time. You definitely made sure it was not boring," Cookie laughed, as she said goodbye to Angie.

"Alright then! Well, I will see you bright and early Monday morning missy. You and Ken drive safely going home," Angie said, as she walked away towards her car.

"Thanks, you too," Ken and Cookie both said in unison.

"I don't know about you, but I could use a hot plate of food. Are you hungry babe?" Cookie asked, knowing that he would have said yes even if he wasn't.

"I'm actually quite hungry myself, but, I wanted to wait to eat dinner with you," he said.

* * *

"Aren't you the perfect gentleman? You're going to love your daddy. Just wait and see," she said, talking to her belly and giving Ken a beaming smile.

Ken looked away for a moment and couldn't believe his eyes. His mind had to be playing tricks on him. He had already grabbed Cookie's suitcase and they were walking towards the gate. He could see a very familiar face in the distance. Melissa. Dammit. He was not ready to see her right now. Not like this. He just had to play it cool and distract Cookie's attention from noticing her. If she did, she would surely want to stop and speak to her.

"Baby? Is that Melissa over there? Ooh this is perfect timing. I know we have our last session with her coming up. I was thinking maybe we could have her over for dinner. What do you think about that?" Cookie asked. She was so enthused and excited to see Melissa.

"Um, I don't know. I guess…" Ken said. Cookie waved high in the air to catch Melissa's attention. Shit. It was too late now. Melissa locked eyes with Cookie first, before noticing Ken.

"Melissa! It's Cookie," she exclaimed.

Ken wanted to dig a hole in the ground right where he stood and disappear. Melissa quickly changed her expression, but he could tell she felt awkward too. "Cookie. Ken. Is that you?" she asked as she was walking towards them. By now, her game face was in full effect. She greeted Cookie with outstretched hands and gave Ken a distant hug; the kind from 8th grade prom when you had to keep six inches of space between you and your dance partner.

● ● ●

"It is so great to see you. What a coincidence. I'm just getting back from a work conference? What about you?" Cookie inquired.

"Small world. I'm actually headed to Virginia for a three-day conference. I'll get to visit with a few girlfriends while I'm there. Hopefully I'll be able to carve out a little fun too," Melissa responded, with her plastered smile still intact.

"That is awesome. Look, Ken and I were just talking about how we would love to have you over for dinner. We can connect when you get back. Thanks so much for everything you have done for us. We can both see the growth in our marriage since we've been coming to you. We truly appreciate it," Cookie said.

Ken was boiling inside. He was angry at Cookie for giving Melissa an invitation to their home without asking him first. Plus, he couldn't believe how fake Melissa was acting in front of her. He did sleep with her after all, against his better judgment or not.

"Oh my, that's really kind of you," Melissa said, shooting a quick, surprised glance over at Ken. She was shocked he would have gone along with something like that. "I would love to. Maybe next Saturday? How does that sound? I'll bring the wine. Consider it my token of gratitude," she said.

"Baby, does next Saturday work for you?" Cookie asked.

"Um, yeah I think that should work. Sounds good to me," Ken replied. Now she wanted his input. Go figure.

"Well, it's set then. Next Saturday it is. Let's shoot for 7:30 pm. I'll prepare something really special," Cookie said, beaming with excitement.

* * *

"Awesome, I can't wait for it. Speaking of food, I'm going to grab a bite to eat before I hop on this flight. Listen, it was so great running into you both. Be safe getting home," Melissa said.

"Thanks, same to you. Hope you enjoy the conference," Cookie replied. Ken just nodded his head and waved goodbye to Melissa. They parted ways as Cookie and Ken stepped outside to walk towards their car.

"Oh my goodness. Babe, I am so sorry. I didn't mean to just invite her over to our house," Cookie said nervously.

"Aw, it's ok baby. You don't have to apologize. I didn't think anything negative about it. I was just surprised, that's all," Ken said.

"What? I can't believe it. No witty comeback sir?" she said.

"You've got jokes, I see. Not at all, babe. I do have a surprise for you though. We're not stopping to pick up food, because I cooked for you. I hope you like it," Ken said. He figured the least he could do was prepare a home-cooked meal for his wife when she got home. He also wanted to soften the blow of telling her about his adulterous one-night stand, any way he could.

"Well, I honestly cannot wait to taste what you have prepared for me. I know it will be delicious. You know, I probably haven't said this enough, but I really want to let you know that I appreciate you for picking up so much of the slack around the house. I feel like my head is out of whack and I'm not pulling my weight. I notice you're doing more and I am so grateful for it," Cookie said.

"Of course, you're welcome baby. You don't have to thank me. That's my job. I love you, so it's easy. Plus, that's what I'm supposed to do," Ken said. His heart pounded faster and faster with each passing minute. His forehead was starting to sweat although the AC was blasting in the car.

"Goodness. Baby, are you hot too? I thought it was just me. Geesh. I am burning up. I guess I'm getting a taste of what menopause feels like. I am so not ready for that. Do you think I will go through menopause?" Cookie rambled.

"Baby. You're just going through a lot of changes with the pregnancy that's all. Plus, I'm sure you won't have any problems with that," Ken reassured her.

They finally pulled into the garage. Ken pulled Cookie's luggage out of the car, while Cookie made a quick hurry to the bathroom. The baby seemed to have more control over her bladder nowadays than she did. She had to pee every 10 minutes; or at least that's how it seemed.

"Hey, the food will be ready in about 20 minutes. Is that ok?" Ken asked. He had all the food pretty much prepared, but still needed to heat up the garlic whipped mashed potatoes in the oven and bake the rosemary chicken a tad bit longer. He also needed to make some spaghetti squash, which he intentionally waited until they got home to prepare.

"Oh sure, that's actually perfect. I was about to ask you if I had time to take a quick shower. I just really want to be comfortable and put my robe on. Thanks baby. I can't wait to taste the food. It smells so good," Cookie replied.

"I hope it tastes as good as it smells. You know I can't let down such a fine cook like yourself. Take your time babe," Ken said,

● ● ●

tapping on the door frame and heading back towards the kitchen. "Oh, did I say fine?" He said, peeking his head back in the door and flashing his million-dollar smile at Cookie.

"You are so silly. I love you. I'll make it a quick shower. The little person and I will be ready for our meal shortly," Cookie replied.

She stepped into the shower and exhaled deeply. The feeling of hot water running over her body never seemed to have felt as good as it did right then. She looked down at her slightly bulging bump. Cookie was so ecstatic about her pregnancy. She didn't want to jinx it, but everything was going well. Even better than she expected. She didn't experience a lot of morning sickness. In fact, Ken was more ill in the beginning than she was.

Sadness suddenly clouded her thoughts. Chelsea never knew the full feeling of being a mother. Maybe if she kept the baby, she would have had a stronger will to fight for her life. Although a deep distrust was wedged between her and her sister in her last days, she still missed Chelsea like crazy. Chelsea crossed her mind every single day. Strangely enough, there were a few days that she didn't think of her mother. She began to weep at the thought of her never being able to be a grandmother.

Cookie didn't want to keep Ken waiting, despite her rollercoaster of emotions. She carefully stepped out of the shower and dried off with their plush, white towels. They were a wedding gift that they both loved. Those towels had to be the softest ones known to man.

Cookie walked towards the bedroom closet to grab her robe. The closet opened with mirrored double doors, with a gracious walk in space. There was no need for them to have a separate closet because this one was literally the size of a bedroom. Ken's clothes were on the left side and Cookie's were on the right. Of course, Cookie's side was fuller. However, Ken was a sneaker lover. He had plenty of assorted colors and styles of sneakers, not to mention several pairs of leather dress boots. They both cleaned up very well when they wanted to (and even when they weren't trying to).

She barely made three steps into the closet when she stepped on a small, plastic cylinder-shaped object on the floor. She heard the contents of it rattle as it rolled under foot. It was more towards Ken's side of the closet. She let out a hard sigh of pain and then bent down to pick up the pill bottle on the floor. She held it up to the light to read the label. Rohypnol. This couldn't be what she thought it was. Her heart started beating rapidly as she looked at the bottle and opened it to see its contents. She could not believe it. Why would Ken even have this? She had to confront him about it. There was no way she would be able to ease her mind without bringing it to his attention.

Cookie slipped on a pair of black lace panties, her pink robe and dropped the pill bottle in her pocket. She felt dirty all over again, putting on the robe. It was one of her favorite gifts from Ken. He got it last Christmas for her. Although it rarely got cold enough outside in Dallas, she still loved to wear it around the house. She had to give him the benefit of the doubt though. There had to be a good reason he had those pills. She just hoped she wasn't making excuses for him living a double life behind her back.

"You are just in time," Ken said, as he placed a bottle of sparkling grape juice on the table. It was the next best thing to a glass of wine for Cookie. They both loved drinking it even before she got

* * *

pregnant. The rest of the food was already set on the table. Ken even prepared a surprise dessert to complement their meal.

"Goodness, this looks so wonderful. Ah, look at you with the sparkling grape juice too. You remembered. You know I love rosemary chicken. Can't believe it's been this long since I've had it. I cannot wait to dig in," Cookie exclaimed.

"Well you don't have to wait any longer," Ken said, as he pulled Cookie's seat out for her to sit down. He said grace for them and they began to dig into their plates.

"Mmm, oh my God. Ken, you have just really outdone yourself. The spaghetti squash is amazing. So are the potatoes. I missed being home. So how was it like being a semi single man for a few days without me?" she joked.

"Well, I missed you a lot. I know that. It's weird, because I always miss you when you're gone. I guess something about having the little person now makes me miss you even more though," Ken responded.

"That's so sweet. Hmmmm. I have a pretty serious question that I need to ask you," Cookie responded curtly.

"Ok, sure baby. What's that? Ask away," Ken responded. What could it be now? He already had enough on his plate trying to confess about Melissa. He really didn't have the mental capacity for additionally awkward conversations.

"Do you mind telling me what this is?" Cookie asked. She pulled the pill bottle out of her robe pocket and placed it in the center of the dinner table. There was an uncomfortable silence for a few seconds. Ken could hear the drip of the kitchen faucet running.

• • •

He must not have turned it off. How could he have been so sloppy? He was going to confess, but not like this. He was supposed to tell Cookie first. Ken didn't want her finding out this way. The pill bottle served as an eerie centerpiece that made their intimate dinner take a sour turn.

"Um baby, it's a really long story," Ken started. He couldn't find the words to move past that point. He gazed into Cookie's eyes and was returned with a cold, piercing stare.

"That's quite alright. I've got all night to hear it," she responded, pushing her plate back and crossing her arms.

"I wanted to tell you myself first. I really don't even know where to start. So, you know how Melissa had my iPod right? I went over there just to get it because she already left the office for the day. She offered me a mimosa. I had one. Got the iPod. We talked for a few minutes. I was supposed to leave right after that," Ken paused.

"Oh, you were planning to go? Let me guess. Is that not quite what happened next? I can't believe her. I can't believe you!" Cookie screamed.

"Please let me finish. The next thing I know, it was morning and I woke up in her bed. I don't remember anything. I promise you. I was so scared and didn't know how to tell you this. Cookie, I really think she put something in my drink. Then I found this pill bottle in her purse. I'm telling you with everything in me that I did not go over there with the intention on sleeping with Melissa. I'm so sorry baby. I ask that you please find a way to forgive me, even if it's not now. I understand if that's the furthest thought from your mind right now," he said.

* * *

"So, let me get this straight. You didn't intend to go over there and sleep with Melissa. But you obviously took one of these pills here, against your own will. Let's not forget that minor detail. Oh and your dick just happened to slip inside of her. Then, to add insult to injury, you slept overnight in her bed? Yes, yes, yes. You also conveniently don't remember a damn thing but picking up that precious little iPod and having a couple of sips of a mimosa?" Cookie ranted. Her veins were popping out of her forehead and her face turned beet red.

"It's not like that Cookie," Ken whispered.

"Then what the fuck is it like, Ken? Come on. Break it down, so it can be forever understood," she cried.

"Baby, I'm telling you..." Ken said, before being sharply interrupted by Cookie.

"Unh unh. I'm not your baby right now," Cookie replied.

"Cookie, I woke up and it felt like a dream. You've got to believe me on this. You know me. I would never cheat on you," Ken said.

"But you did find her attractive. Hell, we both did. I have to give you kudos on that. If you had to step outside the marriage, at least you did it with someone that was remotely some kind of competition for me," she raved, with a slight smirk on her face.

"Who cares? Whether I find her attractive or not is irrelevant. No one is as beautiful as you," he said.

"Ken, let's just say your story is real. Let's say you really did get drugged and had a one-night stand with Melissa that you can't even remember. Please tell me this was not last night," she responded.

"No, it was two nights ago," Ken said.

"I really don't know what to say about this. Let's just finish our meal and try to take this one day at a time. I will be sleeping in the guest room tonight though," Cookie said solemnly.

"No, you're right. I don't deserve to sleep in our bed right now. I'll sleep in the guest room," Ken said.

• • •

Chapter 7

Ken came in the bedroom to say bye to Cookie before he left for work. She was sound asleep and he didn't want to wake her. He kissed her on the forehead and walked out of the door. He barely got two hours of sleep last night. He already felt like the world's biggest jerk for what he did. Now he felt even worse because of the way Cookie found out.

Little did Ken know, Cookie was wide awake when he walked into their bedroom. She heard him coming and just played sleep to avoid speaking to him. She always considered herself to be a desirable woman. Hell, every man she ever dated made her feel like she was the sexiest thing since sliced bread. Now, she felt worthless and more undesirable than ever before.

She decided to go into work a little late, so she could research the pills that Ken hid from her. The conversations she had with Angie at the conference flashed before her eyes. "Girl, all men cheat. The sooner you get that through your head, the better off you will be. You'll save yourself a lot of unnecessary stress too," she could hear her saying in her high pitched, nasal voice.

Cookie remembered her mom even saying it was sometimes ok for a woman to stay after a man cheated. Her father cheated and he was the man she held the highest esteem of respect for. They kept that as a secret between the women of the house. To this day, Cookie didn't think her dad knew that she knew of his adulterous ways. "Baby, love conquers all. Remember that. If it's the right man, you'll find yourself doing all the things you said you would never do. Truth is, you'll find yourself doing the same thing and more for a man that's not worth it too. Know the difference baby. Your heart will always let you know. If it fails, your mind won't steer your wrong. Trust me, I know," her mom told her on her wedding day. However, even her mother thought that Ken could do no wrong. "I hope Chelsea finds a man like Ken one day who can come sweep her off her feet. You girls deserve to be loved and loved well. Are you sure he doesn't have any brothers? A long-lost cousin maybe?" her mom joked. Tears began to stream down Cookie's face as she remembered all the great conversations she had with her mother. She wanted to talk to her mother to yell and cry. She wanted her mother's validation that she wasn't a fool if she decided to stay.

Cookie had to get back to the task at hand though. She opened her laptop and started her Google search by typing in, "Can men be drugged by Rohypnol?" Surprisingly, there were quite a few relevant results. One chat room detailed a comparable situation to Cookie's, except with two men. Next. That one didn't apply to her. She did find something that stated the drug functions similarly to Ecstasy. The kicker is that it often makes the user forget their experience while under the influence of it.

Damn. Now, she was really torn. Based on the information she was reading, Ken may have been telling the truth. She just really didn't know what to believe. Maybe she should call Sheila and talk it out. No. That wasn't a good idea. At least not yet. Sheila was a great friend, but she was also a firecracker. She would exacerbate the situation.

There was only one person she really needed to call. Melissa. She wouldn't call her today since she was probably just getting into the swing of her conference. However, she wanted to call her while Ken's story was still fresh. She had to do it within the next

● ● ●

couple of days. Melissa was a good liar. Hell, she was a woman after all. However, Cookie was nearly certain she knew her well enough to tell whether she was being truthful or not.

Oh well. Her marriage was on the line. She had to play this smart and act quickly. She decided to call Melissa on her way in to work, instead of waiting a couple days. Of course, she was all smiles at the airport yesterday in front of Ken. That was also in public though. She would have to be a damn good faker to act the same way on the phone with Cookie one on one. Now, Cookie hated she even initiated inviting her over for dinner.

She dialed Melissa's number as she rolled to a stop light a few minutes from her job. She was going to control the conversation and didn't need much time to do it. In fact, she didn't want to talk to Melissa long. The possibility of Ken's story being true made her stomach do back flips. The phone rang four times before Melissa finally answered.

"Um, hello. Cookie? Well, what a pleasant surprise. To what do I owe the pleasure of this call?" Melissa asked, with a hurried, yet chipper voice.

"Fake bitch," Cookie thought to herself. Wait. What if Ken was lying to her? She was taking a hell of a gamble. However, she had to stand by her husband; at least for now. "Hey Melissa. Forgive me for calling this early. I know you have your conference and I don't want to interrupt that. I didn't want anything particularly special. Ken and I are so excited to have you over next week. I know we originally agreed on next Saturday, but does next Thursday work instead?" Cookie asked. She didn't confirm with Ken. However, at this point, he just needed to make himself available and deal with it. That was the least he could do for the cost of her loyalty after he betrayed her trust.

"You're fine. You know you can call me any time. I think Thursday will work. Let me just look at my calendar later today and I can let you know for sure," Melissa responded.

"Ok, that sounds great. Ken and I were talking about it last night. We're excited to have the company. He told me he got the iPod back from you. I cannot thank you enough for finding that thing in your office. He keeps it attached to his hip. I'm surprised he even lost it. I call it his mistress," Cookie laughed.

"Of course, I know how men are with their gadgets. I made sure to keep it locked in my office drawer as soon as I saw it. Thankfully, he caught me at the office before I left for this trip. I'm glad he didn't have to go without it for long," Melissa replied.

Cookie took note that Melissa never mentioned Ken coming over to her house. Ken specifically said himself that he stopped by there to pick up his iPod. She was starting to believe her husband more and more. However, she wanted to play it cool for now. Cookie was not going to give Melissa the satisfaction of causing a major scene and abruptly cutting her off. No. She needed to make her conscious perspire a little.

"Yes, that is so true. Well, look, I don't want to hold you any longer. Just wanted to give you a quick call. I hope you enjoy the rest of your conference. I look forward to talking to you when you get back," Cookie said.

"Alright then. I am looking forward to it as well. I can't wait to join you and Ken for dinner. Thanks again for extending the invite

• • •

too. I'll let you know if next Thursday works. You take care Cookie," Melissa said, still in a cool, calm and collected tone.

"Ok, you too. Talk to you soon," Cookie responded, smiling as she hung up the phone.

Melissa was so nervous that her hands started to feel warm and clammy. She couldn't believe how blatantly she violated Cookie's trust by sleeping with her husband. She was still shook up from their random meeting at the airport. This was going to take a while for her to bounce back from. She just had to do everything in her power to keep the secret under wraps.

****

Bill was sitting at home alone, flicking through the channels on TV. He looked outside to check the weather and noticed the clouds were turning gray, just before dusk. He still had a little time to beat the rain. Suddenly, he had a craving for some pizza. There was a small pizza parlor about 15 minutes from home that he and Lisa used to love to go to.

The deep-dish pepperoni, with sausage was his favorite. Bill didn't have to wait long. Surprisingly the restaurant was not nearly as full as it usually was. He could have called it in, but he was prepared to wait. Bill tried not to rush life now. He was much more focused on savoring the moments.

Within 45 minutes he was back home, on the couch, enjoying the first slice of pizza. He started to tear up as he faced the bitter reality that Lisa was not there to enjoy it with him. He was able to accept that she would never come back. However, the memories still hit him with a pang of sorrow at times.

• • •

Suddenly, he heard the doorbell ring. He wasn't expecting any visitors and had the slightest idea of who it could be. He waited for a few seconds and finished his first slice of pizza, before getting up to check the door. He was shocked to see Cathy standing outside. What did she want? Plus, why was she disturbing him now while he was trying to enjoy his food?

"Hello? Cathy? This is a surprise. What brings you here to stop by? Is everything ok?" Bill asked. His tone was polite, but stern. He wasn't really in the mood for company, but he did want to make sure she was ok.

"Oh, yes I'm fine, Bill. I must apologize for stopping by like this. Forgive me, I should have called first. Well, I did, but the number said it was not in service. I must have it listed incorrectly in my phone. Can I come in for a moment? This won't take long. I just have something I want to share with you quickly.

"Oh ok. Sure, come in. It's not a problem at all. Would you like a piece of pizza?" Bill asked, secretly hoping she would say no.

"I'm fine. I don't have much of an appetite right now but thank you. Is that from Ingrid's? I used to love going there. My stomach can't handle many tomato-based foods these days though. I guess that just comes along with the territory, right? Getting older," she laughed nervously.

"Yeah, it is from there. You're not alone. My body isn't what it used to be either. Truth be told, I probably shouldn't be eating this myself. I just had a moment of missing Lisa. We didn't eat out much, but this was one of our favorite pizza places. Can I at least get you some water?" he asked.

"Ok, sure. I'll take some water. Thank you, Bill. I won't hold you long, but I came over to talk to you about Caldwell," she sighed.

"Caldwell? What about him?" Bill's stomach flipped as he relived what Caldwell did to his daughter. His daughter that he could no longer see or hug anymore. He could feel the blood boiling in his veins. What the hell did she have to tell him about Caldwell? He was dead. Honestly, Bill felt no remorse. He got what he deserved.

"I knew some things about my husband. Some nasty, evil things. I stood by him though. You know, marriages from our generation stuck together even if they were hanging on by a thread. Caldwell had another side of him. A sick side. I didn't learn about it until far into our marriage. By then, I felt like I was just too invested to leave. I knew he cheated on me, several times. I never said a word," she said.

"Cathy, you know I hate what happened to Caldwell. I really do. What are you getting at here? I don't really understand," Bill replied.

"Ok, I'm just going to get straight to it. Caldwell had a nasty problem. I thought he was cheating on me with women. Grown women. But he was messing around with little girls. Bill, I'm not sure if you know this but I have a strong feeling that Chelsea was one of those girls. You don't have to tell me if you think so too. I don't claim to know you anywhere near as well as Lisa did. She was your wife. She should know you better than anyone. If you did kill him though, I forgive you. I don't even blame you. If the thought that he hurt Chelsea had even crossed my mind while he was alive, I would have spoken up and said something. If I knew he did something like that to my daughter, I would have killed him too," Cathy said.

63

* * *

Chapter 8

"Hey babe, I'm home!" Sean exclaimed as he walked through the door. He walked in through the garage and there were broken dishes on the kitchen floor. The kitchen light was on, but the living room light was dim. He didn't see Sheila anywhere, so he ran to the bedroom to see where she might be. That's when he saw her sitting at the edge of the bed with her head in her hands. He looked down and noticed some gauzed wrapped around her left ankle.

"Baby, this house. There's something with this house. Maybe it's just me. I'm telling you, I feel this dark presence here. I was about to meet Cookie earlier to get some of that damn dust to put around the doors. I thought I would start preparing dinner first, before you got home. I opened the cabinet and the top four dishes on the stack fell on my head. I still have a bit of a headache. Some of the broken glass must have bounced up and cut me on my ankle," Sheila said with tears streaming down her face.

"What the hell? The plates just came crashing down on your head? Baby, I'm so sorry. Do you feel ok?" Sean asked, putting his bag down on the floor and holding Sheila on the bed.

"Yeah, physically I think I'm ok. I'm about to go meet Cookie in a little bit to get the stuff though. I just can't take it. If there is something on this house, we need to get rid of it fast. There's no way those dishes should have fallen like that. I always push them all the way back in the cabinet. I really don't understand this," she said.

* * *

"I'm so glad you're ok baby. Don't you worry about cooking anything. Let's just stay here and order some food. I'll go clean up the kitchen," Sean said.

"Thanks babe. That's probably a good idea. I'll just call Cookie now and see if I can meet her. She said she would be leaving work around 4:30 pm, so she's probably already home now," Sheila replied.

"Ok, how about something from that new Italian restaurant we tried the other night?" Sean said.

"Oh yeah, that sounds so good. I would love some of that vegetable lasagna again. That was delicious," Sheila said.

"Ok, well I'll wait until you get in touch with Cookie and then I'll order the food when you're on your way back. Unless you think she would be cool with coming here," Sean said.

"I actually thought about that too. She has had enough bad luck. Plus, she's pregnant too. I just couldn't live with myself if something happened. I'll ask her if we can just find a good midpoint. Let me call her now," Sheila said.

"Alright then, baby. I'll be in the kitchen if you need me," Sean said. He walked around the corner and he saw the kitchen light flickering on and off a few times before it stabilized back to its normal brightness. He didn't want to believe their house was haunted by a spirit. Sean didn't want to scare Sheila, but he was even fearful about living in their new home now.

He carefully walked back into the garage to get the broom. As soon as he turned his back, the open kitchen cabinet where the

* * *

dishes fell out of slammed shut. Sean abruptly turned around to make sure his ears weren't deceiving him.

Meanwhile, Sheila was already on the phone with Cookie in the bedroom. The loud slamming of the cabinet startled her. "Hey Cookie, hold on just a sec. Sounds like something is going on in the kitchen," Sheila said.

"Ok, go ahead. I'll be right here," Cookie wanted to help her friend, but she was extremely exhausted from the day. She was torn about whether she should even tell Sheila about Ken's one-night stand. They shared the common belief that friends and relationship problems don't mix, unless either one of them was in a potentially harmful situation. This scenario walked along that line though and she really needed someone to talk to.

"Baby! Are you ok? What's going on?" Sheila asked as she ran into the kitchen.

"Oh, I'm just fine baby. Thanks for checking on me. Sorry about that noise. I was um just closing the cabinet and I guess I let it go too hard. Everything's fine. Did you get in touch with Cookie?" Sean asked, focusing to keep his composure and not let Sheila get worked up again.

"Yeah, I'm actually on the phone with her now. She's on hold. I just came in here to make sure you were ok. I'm about to go meet her at the Home Depot. I won't be gone long," Sheila responded.

"Ok, sounds good. Just text me and let me know when you're on the way back. I'll put the order in for the food then," he said.

"Alright babe. Will do. Let me grab my keys and my purse. I love you. Be right back," Sheila said, kissing Sean on the cheek.

• • •

"Love you too baby. Tell Cookie I said hello," Sean said.

"Alright, will do baby," Sheila said as she closed the door behind her. Meanwhile, Sean was inspecting the rest of the house to see if anything else strange jumped out at him. Although he didn't want to let Sheila know he agreed with her, something was eerie about their home. Plus, Ryan had been quite distant since they moved into the house. He checked on them for about two weeks after they moved. The communication slowly faded soon after.

Sheila was talking a mile a minute on her way to Cookie. However, Cookie had to listen. Despite their rocky relationship at times, Sheila was as close as she would get to a sister outside of Chelsea. In fact, she was closer to Sheila than her own sister. She didn't have the mental capacity to hear about all her woes. Nonetheless, she appeased her friend.

"Sheila, are you absolutely sure you want to use this stuff? You didn't even believe in it when we went to see that gypsy woman. Is it really that bad that now you've gotten a change of heart?" Cookie asked.

"Hell yeah, it's that bad. You try opening a cabinet and have dishes flying at your head. Then, you'll see what I mean," Sheila responded in an irritated tone.

"I'm not minimizing how you feel. Please don't take it that way. I just want you to be careful. Don't go crazy with this stuff. You're only supposed to use a little bit of it. The good thing is you should know immediately if there are some unwelcomed spirits in your house. I think there was something wrong with Chelsea. Like maybe she was possessed or something. I swear, when I started using this stuff, she acted even more strange. I noticed she felt

• • •

very uncomfortable around me though. Then, um, you know what happened shortly after that," Cookie replied, with a cracked voice.

"I'm sorry Cookie. I'm just blabbing my mouth. I'm so sorry. I know you've got to still be missing Chelsea. Something may have been going on, but I know she loved you. That girl was a firecracker. I don't think she liked me much," Sheila laughed.

"You think?" Cookie replied sarcastically, laughing through her tears.

"Oh by the way, I am almost there. About two minutes away," Sheila said.

"Perfect timing. I'm actually pulling up now," Cookie replied. She waited until she saw Sheila pull up to grab the bag of dust from her purse. She was handling it like it was a top-secret weapon. Sheila parked next to her and Cookie got out of the car to greet her.

"Hey girl. You are so beautiful pregnant. I am taking notes! You've got to share your secrets when I get pregnant so I can look as good as you do. Everything ok though? I know when something is up with my girl. Your eyes have a bit of sadness. Maybe it's this damn heat. Goodness, it's hot out here," Sheila said.

"Oh yeah, I'm fine Sheila. Thanks for asking. You're the best. You're right though. Maybe this heat is getting to me. It is hot out here," Cookie said.

"Well, do you have the stuff?" Sheila asked.

* * *

"Goodness, girl. You're going to have these people thinking we are running a drug deal out here. Yes, I have "the stuff"," Cookie laughed.

"Oh yeah. I am going to use this tonight. Wait, where are the instructions?" Sheila asked.

"I couldn't find them, but I remember them very well. Basically, you want to line your front door, any big windows, your garage. Anywhere people can enter your house. Hell, I even used some at work one time. Let me know how it works out for you," Cookie said.

"I will definitely let you know. We need to meet soon about your baby shower too. I have so many ideas. I need to run them by you though and see which ones you like best. There will be time for that though. I'll let you get out of this heat. Sean is ordering some Italian food. Neither one of us felt like cooking after this ordeal. I love you girl," Sheila said, giving Cookie a tight squeeze.

"I love you too. Be careful and call me if anything else weird happens. I'm keeping my fingers and toes crossed that this will be it though. Tell Sean I said hello," Cookie said, getting into the car.

"I will let him know. He thanks you too. Make sure to tell Ken I said hello too," Sheila responded.

Meanwhile, Ken was driving home from work. He was extremely anxious to see Cookie when he got home. He thought about staying a little later at work, but that would only hold off the inevitable. She was likely still upset with him and their interaction was just going to be awkward for a while. He was surprised when

* * *

he pulled into the garage and Cookie's car wasn't there. He barely got in the door when he heard her car pulling up in the driveway. He put his bags down on the floor and exhaled deeply, preparing for Cookie to walk in.

"Hey babe. How was your day?" Cookie asked, as she walked in and placed her purse on the counter.

"It was ok. A little hectic but nothing I was unable to handle. How about yours?" Ken asked. Cookie knew he wasn't too fond of going into details about his day when he first got home. However, he had a feeling he would be doing a lot of things he didn't normally like to do now.

"Um, it was ok. Wasn't too busy thankfully. I was expecting it to be worse than it was. Then, I met Sheila after work. She's convinced that their house has an evil spirit floating around. After talking to her, I can't say I disagree. She called me asking for some of that dust I got in New Orleans from the gypsy woman. I know you weren't too fond of me having it anyway. I gave the rest of it to her," Cookie said.

"That's fine babe. Whatever you want. I can make dinner for us. I have some chicken in the refrigerator that I need to cook anyway. How about that with some quinoa and green beans?" Ken replied.

"You don't have to cook for me every night now. I promise I won't poison your food," she said, with a half serious, half sarcastic laugh.

"Hmmm. I never said that. Baby, I'm truly sorry again. I honestly don't know how it happened. I know it sounds crazy, but I hope you can find a way to believe me," Ken replied. The silence between his last words and Cookie's response seemed like an eternity. He let out a deep sigh and looked down to the floor.

"I believe you, Ken," Cookie uttered softly.

"Huh? Wait. You do? You actually do believe me?" Ken answered, surprised.

"Unless there's a reason why I shouldn't. Yes, I do. Ken, did you ever look up what the effects of those pills are?" she asked.

"No, I just remember grabbing them out of her purse. I felt weird and almost like I was floating in another world. I figured something had to be wrong. I meant to research them, but I hadn't yet," Ken replied.

"Well, you won't have to worry about that unless you just want to satisfy your own curiosity. I looked it up myself this morning. I found a lot of information, but everything basically boils down to it functioning similarly to Ecstasy. One of the main side effects is that it wipes away your most recent memory, including anything that happens to you right after you take it," she said.

"Thank God. I knew there had to be something going on with those pills," he said, feeling relived.

"Yep, looks like you're in the clear. She's still coming over for dinner though. Thursday work for you?" Cookie asked.

"I thought it was next Saturday. Why would we still have her over for dinner after everything that has happened?" Ken asked, with a confused and irritated expression on his face.

"Why not? We can't let this situation ruin our marriage. Let's just have the dinner this one time and eventually just stop talking to her. I called her today and told her we should move it up. I felt it in the pit of my stomach. She played it off well, but I could tell she was lying to me," Cookie responded. Ken could tell her gears were turning and she was deep in thought.

"Ok, if you say so then," Ken responded. He didn't see the sense in Melissa still coming over for dinner. He felt like he had to eat crow though because he technically cheated on Cookie. It didn't matter whether he was coherent for it or not. At least that's how Cookie would see it.

"Ken, please don't make a fool out of me for taking your side on this. I believe you're telling the truth. Don't make me regret my decision," she said, with a piercing gaze that shot straight through to the depths of his soul.

Chapter 9

Thursday came sooner than both Cookie and Ken anticipated. Ken offered to help Cookie with the meal, but she insisted on preparing everything herself. She cooked one of Melissa's favorite dishes: seafood alfredo. She paired it with a fresh spinach salad, including candied pecans, onions, bell peppers, tomatoes and blue cheese. Ken watched in amazement (and concern) as she was going on like nothing ever happened.

"It's almost time. Melissa should be here soon," Cookie said, tossing the salad, while Ken helped her set the table.

"Yeah, it's 7:30 now, so I guess within 30 minutes or so," Ken replied. He felt like he was trapped inside of an episode of *The Twilight Zone*. Cookie was acting too calm and collected, despite her now knowing the truth about how he and Melissa slept together.

Meanwhile, Melissa was just cranking up her car to leave for Cookie and Ken's house. Although she was interested to see how the dinner would go, she wasn't naïve. She couldn't imagine Ken confessing their one-night affair to Cookie. Nevertheless, she also didn't expect their interaction to be peachy king either. She entered their address in her GPS. Siri sounded aloud and said she should reach their home by 7:57 pm. Perfect timing.

A part of Melissa did feel remorseful for what she had done. After all, she had become close with Cookie and genuinely cared for her. This was just one of those moments where she exchanged her deep desires for a visit from karma. Melissa still remembered how moist she felt the first time Ken and Cookie walked into her office. His mysterious persona and quiet strength turned her on;

not to mention his extraordinarily good looks. She replayed the scenario in her mind and tried not to make it obvious how many times she clenched her thighs tightly together. Melissa's thoughts slipped out of reality for a moment as she felt herself getting wet all over again.

She turned on her radio to distract her thoughts. Madonna's "Take A Bow" was on. "Take a bow. The show is over. This masquerade is getting older...," she sang along. She attempted to channel her energy to an innocent dinner with friends. Nonetheless, here efforts were practically useless. She looked down at the clock after the fourth song ended on the radio. She was only three minutes away now. She turned off the radio to clear her head of all the distractions.

Cookie placed the salad on the table and lit the candles to set an extra ambiance. She and Ken just had to wait for Melissa to arrive now. Although Cookie's pregnancy bump was showing, she was still sexier and more beautiful than most women her age (and even younger). Ken could tell she put a little extra in her physical appearance tonight since Melissa was coming over.

The doorbell rang quickly after the table was set. Cookie really wanted to answer the door, but she thought it would be best for Ken as the man of the house to greet her. "Hello Melissa. Great to see you," Ken answered, as he opened the door.

"Great to see you," Cookie mimicked in her head. She clearly had to get her emotions in check. After all, the dinner was her idea even if it was before she found out Melissa fucked her husband. She played it cool though and put on her painted smile as Melissa crossed the threshold to their home. She could have used some of that voodoo dust at that moment.

* * *

"Yes, it's great to see you as well, Ken. I'm sure that wasn't you slaving over the stove for the meal. It smells delicious," Melissa responded, giving Ken a hug.

"Oh, yes it was me. Ken can throw down in the kitchen too. I wanted to set up everything for this grand occasion. We are so honored to have you here. Would you like something to drink before dinner is served?" Cookie asked.

"Water would be lovely. That is just awesome that both of you share the cooking duties. That's my kind of marriage," Melissa laughed nervously.

"Now, don't let Cookie fool you. I cook too, but she is the real chef of the house. I'm positive you are going to love the meal," Ken chimed in.

"Well, hey I'm just honored to be the taste-tester. This is a beautiful home you have here too. It's so peaceful and well decorated," Melissa said.

"Thank you so much. Marriage is about compromise, as I'm sure you already know. I had to pick things that weren't too far on the feminine side," Cookie smiled, sarcastically rolling her eyes at Ken. "Oh, here's your water too. I'm preparing the plates now and dinner will be served in just a few moments. Ken, do you mind putting the other glasses on the table?" Cookie asked.

"Sure, baby. Let me get that for you," Ken replied, briskly making his way into the kitchen.

"Melissa, Tell us about your conference. How was it?" Cookie asked.

* * *

"Oh, you know how those work trips are. So much business. Hardly any time for pleasure. It was nice breaking up the monotony of always being at my office though. I did get to catch up with a couple of friends too. So, that was nice," Melissa replied.

"I understand that. Sometimes it feels like you need a vacation from the work event. Well, let's go ahead and dig in. I remember seafood alfredo is one of your favorite dishes," Cookie said.

"Yes! Cookie this is so thoughtful. Thank you both for inviting me into your home and spending some intimate time together. This is much better than the muffins and strawberries I eat before our sessions," Melissa laughed. The chill was starting to break in the air. However, Ken was still nervous. He was still baffled at how laid-back Cookie was about the whole situation.

"Ken, do you mind saying grace, baby?" Cookie asked.

"Oh yeah, sure. Dear Lord, thank you for bringing us all together this evening on one accord for fellowship, nourishment and let the food be a blessing to our bodies. Amen," Ken said, cautiously opening up his eyes after the prayer.

There were a few moments of silence as everyone started to dig into their food. Melissa was the first to break the silence. "Oh, my goodness. Cookie, this seafood alfredo is phenomenal. I love the sauce. I can definitely tell this is made from scratch," Melissa said.

"Awesome. I am so glad you like it. I must admit, I haven't made it in a while, but I thought this would be a good time to try it again and bring out my cookbook to change it up a bit," Cookie replied.

* * *

"Yes, baby. This is so delicious. You have truly outdone yourself. Even the salad is amazing," Ken said, starting to let his guard down. Everyone was cordially speaking to each other, although their conversation still seemed a bit forced.

"I don't know if it's just me, but the only thing that would make this better is a glass of wine," Cookie laughed.

"In due time," Melissa responded, joining in on the laughter.

"Mmm, wow. I'm feeling a little queasy suddenly. Ken, do you mind wrapping up my plate? I'm going to run to the restroom. I'm sorry Melissa. I'll be right back," Cookie asked.

"Sure, baby. Do you need me to come back with you?" Ken asked.

"Oh no, just keep Melissa company please. I'll be right back," Cookie promised.

Melissa shot a sexy glance over at Ken once Cookie was out of the room. Ken quickly looked away and kept wrapping up Cookie's left overs. "Would you like something else to drink Melissa?" Ken asked.

"I'll take a little more water if you don't mind," Melissa requested.

"I'm going to say this one time and one time only. Bitch, you must have thought you were dealing with a fool. Get up! I want you to turn around and look at me while I'm talking to you," Cookie said, with a gun pointed at the back of Melissa's head. She could see Melissa's shoulders tremble as she stood up slowly and turned around to face Cookie.

Ken was totally caught off guard and didn't think that Cookie would have pulled a gun on Melissa.

"Baby, take it easy now. It's going to be ok," Ken tried to reassure Cookie. However, it was to no avail. She was already too far gone.

"Cookie, I don't know what I did. Where is this coming from? I'm so sorry," Melissa pleaded.

"Sorry? You're sorry for what? Are you sorry for fucking my husband? Is that what you're sorry for? Answer me!" Cookie screamed, still pointing the gun at Melissa.

"Wait. I can explain that. Ken just came by to pick up his iPod. One thing lead to another and...I'm so deeply sorry for betraying your trust Cookie. I hope you can forgive me one day," Melissa cried.

"See, I would believe that. But there's a loop hole in your story. How do you explain these?" Cookie said, pulling the pill bottle from her pocket and slamming it on the table.

"Where did you get those?" Melissa asked, evading Cookie's question.

"I got them out of your purse the next morning after we slept together," Ken chimed in.

"Wait. Why did you go through my purse? Ken, just admit that we both made a mistake and stop trying to pin this on me!" Melissa yelled.

"Whoa. Don't you dare loud talk my husband in my house. You lying bitch!" Cookie said, swinging the gun and hitting the side of

Melissa's face. She really didn't mean to hit her. She only wanted to get the upper hand and scare her; just put her in her place. Nevertheless, Cookie felt damn good hitting her.

"I can't believe this. I didn't…" Melissa sobbed. She stumbled, almost falling to the floor before catching her balance on the dinner table. She held her left cheek in her hand. Melissa kept her hand cradled up to her face.

"No. You did. As a matter of fact, get out my house right now. Yeah, get your shit and get out. You're lucky we don't report your ass and make you lose your job," Cookie replied, following Melissa with the gun as she grabbed her purse.

"Cookie, I'm so sorry. I'm leaving. I'm leaving right now," Melissa said, scrambling out of the front door and running to her car.

Cookie stared at the front door with her gun pointed straight ahead. She stood there for another two minutes but it felt like an eternity. Ken walked up slowly behind her and wrapped his arms around her from behind. He gently pried the gun from her hand and placed it on the counter. Cookie turned around to face him and immediately broke into tears.

"I don't know what came over me. I just don't get it. How could she do that? I didn't mean to do it, I promise. The longer I looked at her, the angrier I became. I just reached my boiling point," Cookie said.

"It's ok baby. You don't have to apologize. I'm so sorry; it's me. I hate all of that even happened. I never meant to hurt you," Ken said.

"I know. It's not you. You have nothing to apologize for. I'm sorry I didn't believe you initially. I guess your wife just still has a lot of baggage even after all this time," Cookie said.

"We all have baggage, baby. It's alright and I'll be here with you through this," Ken said, holding Cookie. He prayed that Cookie wouldn't have another outburst like this. Ken thought that Melissa's life was about to end. He was quite sure that she did too.

Meanwhile Melissa's hands were shaking on the steering wheel the whole way home. At one point she had pulled over on the side of the road and cried, hysterically. She was afraid, angered and embarrassed all at once. Melissa knew that what she did was wrong. However, she didn't expect karma to come back at her like this.

She was paranoid and kept looking in her rearview mirror. Melissa kept looking for Cookie's car, half expecting her to be followed by her. She had been through many compromising situations in her life, but this was by far the worst. She never felt more frightened for her life as she did tonight.

Melissa finally pulled into her driveway at home. She quickly opened the garage door and parked her car inside. She let out a scream inside of the car and prayed no one heard her. Melissa fumbled her way out of the car and walked towards the door that led to the inside of her house. She noticed the door wasn't shut all the way and the knob was damp. She wiped her hands off on her dress and walked inside her home.

The house was always dark inside at night, especially in her kitchen area. She was so flustered, she didn't even bother to turn on the light. She opened the refrigerator to pour herself a glass of wine. Melissa then decided against that as well, drinking the wine straight from the bottle instead. As she closed the refrigerator door, she thought she saw a male shaped shadow standing near her pantry. She shook it off and walked away in the dark. Although she was certain no one was there, she decided to turn on the light switch in her living room just to be safe.

Before she even had the chance to turn on the switch, a hand donning a supple leather glove gently pulled her hand back and behind her back. "Not yet, my dear," the man whispered in her ear.

"What? Wait. Phil, is that you?" Melissa asked nervously. The hot tears rolling down her cheeks felt like molten lava. She was completely speechless and shivering. She knew how much of a loose cannon Phil was, so her best bet was to play by his rules. Melissa had to find a way to save herself though.

"Go ahead. Let's turn on the light now. Slowly. No sudden moves. Can you feel that? Let's just say that's not just me being happy to see you," he laughed, as he placed a sharp blade against the small of her back. Melissa felt powerless as Phil picked up her hand and placed it over the light switch. He flicked on the light and then spun her around.

"Please, Phil. We can talk about this. Whatever has got you troubled, we can work through it," Melissa sobbed.

"We can talk about this," Phil mocked her, sticking his bottom lip out. "Talk is cheap and overrated. Now you have a seat on the couch," Phil said, with a mischievous grin. "What are you waiting for? I said get on the couch, now!" he screamed.

"Ok, I'm here. I'm on the couch. Please don't do this Phil," Melissa cried uncontrollably.

"Isn't it funny how you so called sane people love to say, "Don't do this or don't do that?" I'm sick of playing by your rules and everyone else's. You try to act like you're so innocent and perfect. I saw that married guy coming out of your house the other day. I've been watching you for a while. I love watching you. He's quite the looker, isn't he? You just couldn't stay away from him even though he was married, could you?" Phil snickered.

"Phil, that wasn't what it seemed. I promise," Melissa replied.

"It wasn't what it seemed, huh? Well it seemed like he came here, banged your brains out, spent the night and left the next morning. How did it feel? Do you have even the slightest inkling of remorse? I bet the thrill made you climax like never before. I know you better than he does; better than anyone. I know your habits, your favorite perfume. I know where you like to shop and your favorite foods. I loved you. I did. You were just too damn blind to see it. Go ahead. This is the part when you lie and say, "But wait Phil. I've loved you too for all this time. Let's run away together," he said in a softer, hushed tone.

Melissa couldn't utter a word. She was completely traumatized by the series of events that transpired tonight. She slowly glanced towards her bedroom door. The distance from the couch to her bedroom was just long enough that he may be able to catch her if she tried to run away. What did she have to lose? He seemed like he was going to harm her either way. At least if she ran, she would have a better chance of escaping unscathed. Melissa darted off the couch at lightning speed, but Phil was immediately on her heels.

* * *

She kept running for what seemed like an eternity until she finally reached the bedroom door. She made it inside just in time, but not quickly enough to close and lock the door behind her. Phil grabbed her from behind and put her in a choke hold with his right arm, just over her bed. He moved his left arm to slide the blade across her throat. She writhed and squirmed like a fish out of water. He sighed deeply and chuckled as her limp body fell on the bed. Blood quickly began to pool all over the mauve colored comforter.

Chapter 10

Ken was sleeping so hard that he totally slept through his first alarm. Friday. Yes, he was so glad the weekend was almost here. Last night's ordeal wore him and Cookie out. He faintly heard a phone ringing in the background. However, he thought it must have just been part of his dream. Then he saw Cookie's phone flashing and illuminating the room. He looked over at his phone to check the time. 6:04 am. Who could be calling her this early?

"Baby, I'm sorry to wake you up but your phone was just ringing," Ken said, softly nudging Cookie's shoulder to wake her up.

"Huh? What? Is she still here?" Cookie asked.

"What are you talking about baby? Do you mean Melissa? No, she practically was running out of here last night. It's ok baby," Ken answered.

"Whew. Ugh, how could I forget? I am so embarrassed. I can't lie. It felt so good holding that gun to her head and watching her plead for her life. Did my phone just ring?" Cookie asked.

"Yeah, it did. That's why I was trying to wake you up," he said.

"Oh, ok. I'm sorry. Let me see. Ah, it was Sheila. That's unlike her to call this early," Cookie said, dialing her voicemail to hear Sheila's message.

"Babe, is everything ok?" Ken asked, reading Cookie's perplexed expression on her face.

She motioned her hand towards him quickly, flinging it back and forth. "The remote. Is it in on your side? Hand me the remote," Cookie said frantically.

"Let me see. Ah, yeah here it is. It fell on the side of the bed," Ken said.

"Let me see it," Cookie said, nearly snatching the remote out of Ken's hand. She immediately turned on the TV and stopped when she got to the news report on Channel 13.

"We will have more on this story as we gain development on it. Melissa Henton, a prominent counselor and psychiatrist in the DFW metroplex was found murdered in her home early this morning. The murder is predicted to have happened sometime between 9:00 pm last night and 2:00 am this morning. No details yet on a suspect or motive, but this is truly a sudden and tragic loss. Tom, back to you," the news reporter said.

"Oh my God. I can't. Goodness, I can't believe this. Excuse me," Cookie said as she ran to the bathroom to vomit. Now, she felt horrible for what she did to Melissa. Although she was in the wrong for sleeping with Ken, she never actually wanted to wish death on her.

"You've got to be kidding me," Ken whispered, still lying in bed.

Cookie walked out of the bathroom into the vanity area by the sink to brush her teeth and rinse her face off. "Well, that's definitely not the way I expected to start off the morning," she sighed.

"Wait. Sheila knows Melissa too?" Ken asked.

* * *

"Not exactly. She only knows of her through me. She must have remembered her name though. She was telling me about the whole Ryan situation with him being skeptical of them having the house they're in now. We were talking about the news article that got posted that night of the Christmas party," Cookie responded.

"Ryan. That's right. I know he's going to be torn up when he hears about it, regardless of whatever volatile history they had," Ken said.

"Yeah, you're right about that. I didn't even think about Ryan. I know Sheila is probably over there flipping out. I'll call her back on my way in to work," Cookie said. She stared at herself in the mirror as she brushed her teeth and prepared to take a shower. She exhaled deeply. Today was going to be a long and eventful day.

****

"Hello? Girl, did you get my message?" Sheila shrieked as soon as she answered the phone.

"Yes, I did. I saw it on the news too. I just can't believe it. I literally just saw her last night. She was over at our house for dinner," Cookie said.

"Wow, are you serious? I can't believe that. I know that's got to be a creepy feeling. Goodness," Sheila sighed.

"Well, there's something else I need to tell you about last night. I don't even know how to go into this. Jesus," Cookie said.

"Don't tell me she tried to push up on Ken. That floozie. I will cut her ass," Sheila exclaimed.

"You are too much. Let's just say that if we were playing hot and cold, you'd be pretty damn hot," Cookie admitted.

"Oh no. Cookie. Please don't tell me that Ken....Did he sleep with her?" Sheila asked, removing all playful inuendo.

"Well, it's complicated. I never thought I would be one of those women who made excuses for her husband cheating, but here I am. Life has made a fool out of me. So, he did sleep with her. However, it wasn't totally his fault. She slipped something in his drink," Cookie said, before she was abruptly cut off by Sheila.

"Wait a minute. Is that what he told you or is that what you know to be true?" Sheila asked in a concerned tone.

"Both. He told me. He said he couldn't hold it any longer. It happened while I was on my trip. He left his iPod at her office. She held on to it for him. She poured him a drink while he was there. One thing led to another. You know the drill. The weird part though is he found the drugs in her purse," Cookie said.

"What was he doing in her purse? Did he suspect something was wrong?" Sheila asked.

"Basically. He doesn't even remember having sex with her. He woke up feeling groggy in her bed the next morning. I guess that's what prompted him to look inside her purse," Cookie said.

"Cookie, I'm sorry. Seriously. At least he didn't do it on purpose. You know I'm always on your side, but I just can't see Ken deliberately doing anything like that. Either that or he's the best

* * *

damn liar I've ever seen. I can't help but to ask though. Why in the hell was Melissa at your house for dinner last night after all this?" Sheila said.

"I didn't find out about everything until after I had already invited her over. I just kept everything status quo, like nothing happened," Cookie replied calmly.

"Well, kudos to you. I'm a lot of woman but I don't know who I would have had to be to let that tramp sit down at my dinner table. I just couldn't do it. You are good girl. There are going to be so many jewels in that crown of yours when you get to heaven," Sheila joked.

"Um, that's not all though," Cookie said softly.

"What could possibly top that? I feel like I'm watching an episode of Jerry Springer. This is too much," Sheila said, devouring all of the details from Cookie.

"I went back into the bedroom and acted like I was going to the restroom. I went to go get my gun while she was still eating. I left her alone in there with Ken. Came back in the kitchen with that gun pointed right at the back of her head. I told her to get up and face me. Look me in the eye like a real woman and own up to what she had done. She just stood there crying profusely. I hit her in the face with the gun too. That part was by accident, but I'm so ashamed now. It felt good at the time, but I really did a horrible thing," Cookie cried.

"Candice, I'm calling you by your real name so you can hear me when I say this. I'm not trying to kick you while you're down, I promise. What were you thinking? You have another life that you're carrying now. I get what she did was foul. But that could have really gotten ugly last night, and the blood would have been all on your hands. I'm concerned about you," Sheila said.

"I know it wasn't right. I just felt like I had to get back at her somehow and let her know I'm not a fool. I really regret it now that she's dead though. Who would have done something like this?" Cookie asked rhetorically.

"I'm sure it will all surface soon. Keep your head up though and try not to let this get to you. You have a life in there that you must worry about. I love you," Sheila replied.

"I love you too. Thank you for being there through everything and not judging me. I can imagine I sound like such a nutcase sometimes. You've never walked away from me though. That means more than you could ever know," Cookie said.

"You know I'm here forever. There is no getting rid of me. You are my ride-or-die sister. Now, cut it out with all the mushy stuff before you have my makeup running," Sheila laughed, as her voice cracked.

"I know, right. Ok, well I'll talk to you later then," Cookie laughed.

"Alright, sounds good. Talk to you later," Sheila said, before hanging up the phone. She was getting ready for a meeting she had with a client who wanted to have her cater a 50th birthday party. She was really excited about the possibility of the deal, since it would bring in some great revenue for the month. September was usually a slow month, so this would help balance things out until the Thanksgiving rush.

* * *

Sheila could smell bacon sizzling on the stove. She knew Sean was up getting ready for work, but she didn't think he had enough time to cook her breakfast. She was slightly irritated that he was cooking bacon though, because she recently tried removing it from her diet. Nevertheless, she was going to eat it today. She couldn't resist that smell.

"Hey baby, I made some breakfast for you. It will be ready in a couple of minutes. Pancakes, eggs, bacon and grits and some freshly squeezed orange juice from these two hands," he said, walking up behind Sheila and placing his hands at the top of her thighs, near her groin.

"Mmm that breakfast sounds delicious. This is a pleasant surprise. I can't wait to taste it. I hope it doesn't put you behind on your day," she said.

"Not at all. I was planning on getting into the office a little later this morning anyway. This worked out perfectly. Were you able to get in touch with Cookie to tell her about the counselor?" Sean inquired, rubbing her legs and the sides of her hips.

"Yeah I actually just got off the phone with her. She's pretty shook up about it. Most of the conversation was me trying to calm her down," Sheila said.

"Wow, I can imagine. That had to be a huge shock for her. I'm sure she still appreciated you calling to tell her," he said.

"She really was. Alright now. If you keep rubbing on my legs like that, we won't make it to the breakfast table," she smiled, putting on her lipstick.

● ● ●

"Who says the kitchen is off limits? I have you on the menu for breakfast too," he sneered, with a mischievously sexy grin.

"Well I guess it's not then. Let's see how much time I have here. We'd better make this a quick feast then," Sheila responded, grabbing Sean by the hand and leading him towards the kitchen.

"The way you're looking right now, I won't last too long anyway baby," Sean said, giving her a smack on her supple behind.

"Mmmmm, baby this smells so good. You have truly surprised me today. Look at you being romantic in the kitchen," she replied.

"Anything for my baby. Now, let's dig in," he said, winking his eye at her and mentally undressing her. Her black laced bra and panties left little the imagination, but her body was spectacular. Sheila had the kind of physique that would easily turn any man's head.

Sean pulled out Sheila's chair and walked over to the counter to pour her a glass of orange juice. They both ate quickly, as Sheila praised him for the excellent meal. Sheila heard her cell phone ringing from the bedroom and looked at the kitchen clock on the wall. "I still have time. I wonder if that's them calling me now," she uttered nervously.

"Baby, what time is your meeting again?" Sean asked.

"Well it's at 9:00. But you know how this traffic can be sometimes," she said.

"It's ok. It's only 7:30 now. You're meeting with them at the business right? That's only 15 minutes away," he reminded her.

* * *

"Yeah, you're right baby. Thanks for keeping me calm. I'm just a little anxious about it that's all," she admitted.

"Would you like some more orange juice baby?" Sean asked. Obviously, he was totally disregarding her concern about being late to the meeting. Sean had one thing on his mind. Truth be told, she wanted it just as badly, if not more, than he did.

"Oh sure, that orange juice was so delicious. Everything was. I've been so on the go lately, I've been slacking about eating breakfast sometimes. Thank you for looking out for me," Sheila said.

"That's what I'm here for. You always do so much for me. It's my pleasure to serve you. Do you mind tilting your head back?" he asked. Sheila was clearly caught off guard, as she had a perplexed look on her face.

"Um, sure. What are you up to Mister?" she smiled, as she did exactly as he requested.

"Open your mouth," Sean demanded. Melissa tilted her head back slowly, as Sean slowly poured the last of the orange juice from the pitcher in her mouth. Some of it spilled at the top of her breasts. He quickly licked up the orange juice and traced his tongue up to her neck and then to her mouth, giving her an aggressive open-mouthed kiss. He tasted the orange juice with her as he lifted her up by her waist and carried her over to the kitchen counter.

Sean pulled her lace panties to the side and started tasting her slowly at first. Then he made quick, short laps around her clitoris with his tongue. She wrapped her legs tighter around his neck

* * *

with each lick. He stimulated her senses so sharply, that she had to push his head away from her.

"Now, why would you push me away like that baby?" Sean said, looking up at Sheila from his kneeled position on the kitchen floor.

"I'm not pushing you away. I just want this," she said, sliding down his boxer briefs and lifting one leg up, around his back. She felt his steel like manhood slide inside of her wet valley. Sean nearly broke her bra trying to rip it off her. She helped him and threw it on the kitchen table. It landed right on top of the pancake syrup bottle. She started moving faster and harder, grinding on his pelvis so hard they could feel their bones bumping against each other.

"You're not right. Why does it have to be so good baby? You know I can't last long when you do that move. Oh. Oh. Damn baby. Wait. Slow it down or I'm about to.....agh!! Yes!! Um hmm. Don't you go anywhere. Let me hold it in you for a little while longer," Sean said. Seeing him so satisfied turned Sheila on even more. They nearly climaxed in unison as she pulled her legs around him as tightly as she could. She wanted to feel every inch of him spilling over inside of her. Sheila didn't want to waste a drop.

She leaned her head back and laughed. "Mmmm, well good morning to me. Thanks for the wonderful meal baby. Oh, and that juicy breakfast sausage too," Sheila said.

"It's my pleasure. Thank you for bringing the extra hot cakes. I aim to please," he grinned.

* * *

Chapter 11

Ken's work day flew by much quicker than he anticipated. In fact, he needed it to slow down so he could check everything off his to do list. However, he welcomed a lunch break to clear his mind from Melissa's death. His coworker Lawrence wanted to join him for lunch, but he lied and said he had an errand to run. He would have been open to it any other time, but he really needed the time alone to clear his mind.

Almost as soon as he sat down in the SUV, his phone rang. He was very surprised to see that it was Bill. Although Bill and Ken had a great relationship, he never just called him directly. Ken answered, afraid Bill might be calling for something serious.

"Well, this is a nice surprise. Hey Bill. How is life treating you? It's so good to hear from you," Ken said.

"Oh, I'm hanging in there, son. Taking it one day at a time. Listen, I saw this report on the news about a woman who got murdered in cold blood inside of her own home. It was right there in Dallas. I haven't talked to you and Cookie in a while, so I just want to make sure you both are safe. Plus, I know you'll tell me the truth if something is wrong with Cookie," Bill laughed.

"Wrong? Oh there's nothing wrong at all. She's just busy with work and her hormones are a little out of whack. That's all," Ken replied, as he pulled out of the parking garage. He didn't want to be rude, but his mind was preoccupied on a quick but tasty place to have lunch. There was that new Panda Express around the corner. He decided to go there. He would just suffer the consequences for tomorrow's work out when it came.

"Ok, well I'll take your word for it if you say so then," Bill responded in an authoritative tone.

"I appreciate you checking on us. I know Cookie will be so thankful. I'll have to tell her that I talked to you. As for the murder, Cookie and I did hear about it. That's a truly sad fate for that lady. I just don't understand how anyone could do something like that," Ken replied. He felt like it was wise to leave out the fact that Melissa was their marriage counselor. He didn't think Cookie divulged that information with her father.

"Oh no. You don't have to bother her. I'll talk to her in her own time, I'm sure. Although it has been a few days since I've heard from her. I take that back. Have her call me."

"How is that grandbaby doing? I think I've picked up some of Lisa's sentimental ways since she passed. I just can't wait," Bill replied, smiling on the other end of the phone. He felt a lump in his throat as he thought about Lisa not being able to meet her grandchild.

"I'll have to take a picture of her tonight and send it to you. We are still waiting to find out the sex of the baby. We want it to be a surprise. About four more months and he or she will be here. We are really ecstatic about it too," Ken grinned. He just pulled into the parking lot at Panda Express, but he decided to stay in the car until he finished talking to Bill.

"Ah, I see. Four months is no time. Although I can't say I understand this new aged way of thinking. I mean, don't you want to know what the sex of the baby is, so you can tell people what kind of gifts to get? Seems like it would just make it easier

* * *

on the both of you," Bill asked, with a perplexed tone of concern in his voice.

"Well, we did talk about it but we both agreed we want to be surprised. We figured that yellow was a safe neutral color for gifts," Ken laughed.

"Hey, well suit yourselves. I'm just excited for my first grandchild. I can't wait. But, look who's talking. I'm sure you can't either," Bill said.

"Yes, I'm very excited about becoming a dad, especially with Cookie. I'm counting down the days," Ken replied.

"I'll let you get back to it. It was good talking to you Ken. Hopefully I'll get to see you and Cookie before the baby gets here. Love you both," Bill replied.

"Love you too Bill. I'll talk to you later," Ken smiled, as he hung up the phone. Bill wasn't really an affectionate guy. He came from the generation of men who rarely expressed their feelings because it just wasn't the thing for men to do. So, it was a big deal for him to say he loved them both. Ken truly looked at Bill like his own father and really valued their relationship.

Ken walked into Panda Express, surprised that there wasn't a long line. He was initially planning on taking the food to go, but he decided to eat there instead. The waitress started making flirtatious eye contact with him as she asked to take his order. "Ok, so that will be one Kung Pao Chicken and an egg roll, with a Sprite. Is that all you need? I'd be happy to get you anything else you want," she said with a sexy smile.

The waitress was actually very attractive. She had to have been in her mid-20s. Ken kept his conversation firm and direct. He couldn't let himself get caught up in another infidelity situation, even if the first one was somewhat against his own will. "No, thank you. That will be all," Ken replied.

"Ok, sounds good. Well, I'll have the food right out for you," she said. The waitress matched his curt tone and quickly walked back into the kitchen.

"Thanks," Ken replied. He was sure she heard him, but she was nearly already in the kitchen before he could finish uttering the word. He grabbed a fortune cookie and took a seat at a table on the left side of the restaurant, facing the door.

Ken started browsing through his phone on Facebook and saw a recent picture of Charles, Alicia and Lance together. It looked like a new family portrait. They were a beautiful family. Charles and Alicia were meant for each other. They even finished each other's sentences sometimes; it was weird yet refreshing to see. Lance was just a big ball of fun. That kid never saw a sad day. Every time Ken saw him, he was always laughing and playing. Goodness, he had really grown. Time certainly does fly by. Ken clicked *like* on the picture. Then he went back and clicked the *love* button instead.

The waitress quickly turned the corner and placed the food on his table. "Here's your food," she said, sliding it on the table just before bumping his hands. "Let me know if you need anything else," she said. She walked off before Ken could respond.

Ken just laughed to himself and started eating his food. Some of the memories were now coming back to him about the night with

Melissa. This sure was an inopportune time for that, now that she had been murdered. He remembered her grinding on top of his lap, while he reached up to grab her full, supple breasts (or at least as much as he could hold in each hand). He looked out of the window in front of him to try shaking the thought out of his head. Ken was always a quick eater, but he paced himself a little slower today. He honestly dreaded going back into the office. Ken really wasn't in the mood to keep putting on a face like everything was ok.

He opened his fortune cookie as he stood up to throw his trash away. He never really believed in them, but always thought they were fun to read. "Karma will soon come to collect," the fortune said. Ken just shrugged it off as a meaningless statement. He figured that several of the cookies probably had the same fortune inside.

****

Meanwhile, Phil was at home, blasting his stereo and cooking a frozen pizza in the oven. He decided to go in his guest room and complete the project he had been working on. He skipped down the hallway, to the beat of the music as he sang along, "Ooh! Here I go again. Falling in love all over. Ooh! The cycle never ends. You just pray you don't get burned," he crooned in an off-key tone.

He grabbed the pink velvet coat he bought from the thrift store and draped it over the mannequin. He buttoned the top two buttons at the bottom and left the rest undone. He wanted the mannequin's breasts to be nearly exposed. Then he teased the crown of the mannequin's auburn wig with his fingers. Something was still missing. He added a picture that he printed from Facebook of Melissa and stapled it to the mannequin's forehead.

His dog, a beautiful golden German shepherd, came gracefully trotting in the room to see what all the fuss was about.

The dog started barking after a few seconds of staring intently at Phil sing, dance and dress the mannequin all at once. "What are you looking at? Shut the hell up Ralph! Can't you see I'm working?" Phil said, throwing a stack of old mail in the dog's face. He jumped back, turned around and then quickly trotted out of the room.

"Now, where were we, my sweet?" Phil asked. There were many photos of Melissa plastered around the room for him to choose from to place on the mannequin. Phil had built himself a shrine of sorts in his guest bedroom for Melissa. He rarely had any visitors. If he did, no one was ever allowed to go in that room. He kept it locked with a special key whenever he was away or not in the house alone.

Although they were not friends on Facebook, Phil found a way to hack into her account. He always enjoyed reading her private messages. He even received an alert every time she posted. They could have been together at that very moment if she had just cooperated and went with the flow.

Phil put the finishing touches on the mannequin. Then, he took a bottle of Melissa's perfume that he stole from her house and sprayed it all over the mannequin. He inhaled deeply and smiled wide as he took in the essence of the fragrance. It was as if Melissa was standing right next to him. He grabbed the mannequin's right breast, imagining it was Melissa's. Just then,

* * *

he heard a loud knock at the door. He turned down the music and walked slowly to towards the living room. He wasn't expecting anyone to visit him.

He looked through the peephole and saw a police officer standing at the door. Ralph slowly walked into the living room and stood behind Phil, sniffing the side of his leg. Phil ran his fingers through his hair one time and exhaled deeply, before opening the front door. The officer was just about to knock for a second time.

"Hello officer. May I help you with anything?" Phil offered in a chipper tone.

"Yes, I think so. Hi, I'm Officer Lake. Is this Phil Talsky's residence?" Officer Lake responded, extended his right hand for a hand shake.

"Yes, you're looking at him," Phil replied with a forced smile. He reluctantly shook Officer Lake's hand.

"Do you happen to know a Melissa Henton by chance?" the officer asked. Phil gave a perplexed expression back to the officer before he answered.

"Well I know a lot of people officer. I can't say that name rings a bell though. I would need a little more information. Maybe a face or a something. I've always been much better with faces than names," he smiled. Phil rubbed Ralph's head as the officer prepared his rebuttal. He was sweating bullets but remained on guard because he had no idea what would happen next.

"I see. I understand. I never forget a face either. Do you mind if I come in for a second?" the officer asked.

• • •

"Oh sure, my house is such a mess. If you don't mind that, then yes, be my guest. Come on in," Phil answered.

"Great. Thank you for your cooperation. You should see my house. If it weren't for my wife, it would hardly ever stay clean," Officer Lake said.

"Women. Can't live with em. Can't live without em, right?" Phil laughed.

"Exactly, you're spot on about that. I smell a faint hint of perfume. I'm not interrupting anything, am I?" Officer Lake questioned, in a light-hearted tone.

"Oh no. Now, a few days ago, that would have been a different story. I guess her scent is still lingering in here a bit. May I get you some water, orange juice, vodka? I'm sorry for the vast, yet limited array of options," Phil smiled.

"Oh no, I'm just fine. Thanks for asking," Officer Lake said. He didn't totally buy Phil's explanation for the perfume, but he let it ride.

"Sure. If you'll excuse me for a moment, I think I'll pour myself a glass of orange juice," Phil said.

Officer Lake quickly surveyed the living room but kept an eye on Phil's every move. He noticed a sharp blade half hidden under a stack of mail. It looked far too fancy to be a letter opener, but just right for gutting a fish. Better yet, maybe even a human.

"Do you mind if I use your restroom for a moment, Phil?" Officer Lake asked.

● ● ●

103

"Of course, it's the first open door, down the hall and to your right," Phil answered without obviously looking in Officer Lake's direction. However, he was closely watching his every move.

Officer Lake really did have to use the restroom, but he also felt something was suspicious about Phil. He was washing his hands when he noticed a tattered photo, peering underneath the wrong he was standing on. He picked up the photo to examine what it was. A picture of Melissa. He instantly recognized it as soon as he saw it. He knew it was time to make a move with Phil.

"Listen, I don't want to waste too much of your time here. but this is a picture of Melissa I found on the floor in your restroom. After seeing this, are you sure you don't know her?" Officer Lake said, showing him the picture as he walked into the living room. Phil was all too familiar with the photo. Little did Officer Lake know, it was one of his favorite pictures of Melissa. It was one of many that he had hanging up on the ceiling of his guest room. He must have been careless and left another copy of it laying around.

"I can't say that I do. Why do you ask? Whoever she is, I hope she's ok. The lady in the photo is an old girlfriend of mine. Guess I forgot to purge all the memories," Phil replied. Ralph walked towards Officer Lake and started sniffing around his feet. "Ralph! Stop that. Leave him alone, please. Bad dog," he slapped his knee as he summoned for Ralph to come next to him.

"It's quite alright. He's fine. Melissa died earlier this week. She was murdered. She didn't seem to have any enemies, so we're just trying to get down to the bottom of it all," he said.

"Oh my God. Well, if there is anything I can do to help solve the case, I am all for it," Phil replied.

"That's really great to know. Does that car parked outside belong to you?"

"Of course, that's my car. Officer, with all due respect, I really have some business I need to tend to. I don't see the relevance of some of these questions you're asking," Phil replied, clearly showing his agitation.

"As you can imagine with a case like this, there are a lot of moving parts. Everything is considered a viable piece to the puzzle until we can get some concrete evidence," Officer Lake responded calmly.

"Ok, so exactly how do I fit into this puzzle?" Phil asked, more aware of his tone this time.

"Melissa's neighbor across the street reported sounds of screaming when we asked her about her knowledge of the night of the murder. She said she didn't see anyone but she did get a view of the license plate of someone who left her house after midnight. That license plate matches yours exactly. Was anyone driving your car this week, specifically on Thursday evening?" Officer Lake asked.

Phil took a brief pause to collect his thoughts before he answered. "Wait a minute. So you mean to tell me that the only "puzzle piece" that led you here is some woman who thinks she saw my car in the middle of the night? I'd say it might just be time to go back to the drawing board. Don't you think, Officer Lake?" Phil smirked sarcastically.

"Everything and everyone is fair game until we get to the bottom of this. Melissa was brutally murdered. This is clearly a heartless crime that we must take seriously. I noticed something else, though. I promise, I'll be on my way shortly," Officer Lake said.

"What would that be?" Phil responded, taking a sip of his drink.

"Is this knife that you have here a letter opener of sorts? It looks like it can do some severe damage," Officer Lake inquired.

"I like to go fishing sometimes. I use it to cut my bait, chop down weeds and just odds and ends around the house. Let me guess. You must think it's an accessory murder weapon for Melissa's case," Phil asked, with a sarcastic smirk forming at the corners of his mouth.

"The weapon wasn't found at the crime scene. However, judging by the size of that blade you have here, that could have easily fit the bill. It's probably just all a big coincidence. I'll be leaving now. Thank you for your time Phil and my apologies for any disturbance to your day," Officer Lake replied.

"Wait. Officer Lake, before you leave, I do have one thing that you probably should know," Phil said.

Officer Lake didn't trust Phil. He subtly placed his hand on his holster before he turned around to fully face him. "Oh yeah. What's that?" he said, looking Phil dead in his eyes.

"This!" Phil replied, flinging the gun he was holding in the back of his pants and firing it at Officer Lake. He clipped him just above the shoulder, right before Officer Lake shot him in the knee and then in the bicep. Phil couldn't hold on to the gun any longer.

* * *

106

Officer Lake grabbed his arm, as he called for backup. Meanwhile, Phil laid on the floor cursing and moaning in agony.

"This is Officer Lake. I've been shot. I'm here at 5762 Loyal Cove Ln. Suspect is down. I fired twice. He's hit. Get here quickly," he said.

* * *

Chapter 12

"This is Sylvia Rosharon reporting live here, near downtown Dallas. Tonight, the family and friends of Melissa Henton can close a chapter to their grief. Phil Talsky, who we have since learned was a client of Ms. Henton's therapy practice, has been taken into custody by officials this evening. He is also believed to be linked with two other murders of women in the Dallas area in the last six months. This is a tragic story of a full life that ended too soon. Rena, back to you," the news reporter said.

"Babe look at this. They found Melissa's killer," Ken said.

"What? Who was it? Did they say?" Cookie asked, with a wide-eyed expression on her face, coming out of the bedroom.

"Apparently he used to see her too. That's crazy. You just can't trust anyone these days," Ken replied.

"I know. I'm still so embarrassed at how I reacted that night. I just wanted to teach her lesson, but I shouldn't have done that," Cookie confessed.

"I know baby. Although, you did have me fooled for a minute though. I could have used a dress rehearsal before that," he laughed.

"Oh shut up. Who asked you?" she laughed back at him.

"You know what? I thought it was kinda sexy though. You taking control like that and looking so beautiful while you did it," he said, leaning in on the couch to give her a kiss. Ken still found her very attractive during her pregnancy. She had a glow that he had never seen before. He was more than elated that she was carrying his child.

"Is that so? Hmmm, maybe I should find somebody else to slap around and pistol whip then," she said. "Ah, ooh that didn't feel too good," Cookie said, suddenly grabbing the bottom of her foot.

"Give me your foot babe. I'll rub it out for you," Ken said, putting her left foot in his lap. Cookie exhaled deeply, as she took in every stroke of his big, strong hands rubbing her foot.

"Thank you so much baby. I swear that wasn't a ploy for a massage. That was a weird feeling. Like a shooting pain in my foot out of nowhere. I don't know what that was about. Guess I'll blame that on being pregnant too," she smiled.

"I didn't think you were trying to make a plot for me to rub your feet. I'm doing it because I love you and I want you to feel good," Ken said.

"I can't deny it feels like heaven. This is relieving so much tension in my feet, it's unreal. Have you heard back from Charles yet about when he and Alicia and Lance are coming to visit us? It will be good to get it in now before it gets too close to the due date. Besides, I miss seeing them. It's been a while. Lance is so cute too. I guess I better not call him cute now that he's getting older," Cookie said, with a genuinely wide smile spread across her face.

"Thanks for reminding me babe. I need to call him back. Maybe next Saturday night. How does that sound?" Ken replied.

"Awesome. Let's do it. Saturday it is. They may as well spend the night too. It will be nice to have some extra company anyway," she said.

"I know Lance would love that. I'll text Charles now and let him know. I'll let you know what he says," Ken responded.

"Ok, baby. Thank you for the massage too. That was so nice. I feel like I'm walking on clouds now," Cookie said.

"I aim to please. I'm glad baby. Now give me some sugar," he said, leaning in to kiss Cookie on the lips. She smiled and leaned forward to meet him halfway. "Now, let me give the baby a kiss too," Ken continued.

"I love you. I can't wait to see you as a father. You are going to be amazing. I know it," Cookie said.

"Thank you, baby. Just like I know you are going to be an excellent mother," Ken replied, rubbing her shoulder.

"That really means a lot that you think so. I have such a sweet tooth suddenly. I'm going to get some of the ice cream out of the freezer. Do you want anything?" Cookie asked.

"Oh no, I'm fine baby. Thank you for asking," Ken replied.

"Can you believe we just have three more months until we see this little bundle of joy? It just doesn't seem real. But I guess I have the belly to prove it, right?" Cookie laughed, looking down at her protruding baby bump.

● ● ●

"Yes, I cannot wait. I'm so excited. I forgot to tell you I talked to your dad. You may want to call him when you get a chance. Nothing urgent. He just wants to hear your voice," Ken said.

"I'm such a bad daughter. I haven't talked to him in a while. Ok, thanks for letting me know. I'll call him. How did he sound when you talked to him?" Cookie inquired.

"He sounded good. He's just excited to be a grandfather. Hey, do you regret us waiting to find out the sex of the baby?" Ken asked.

"No, that's what we agreed on. Why do you ask that, babe? Do you regret it?" Cookie asked.

"Not at all. I feel the same way. Let's just say your dad is really anxious to know the sex of the baby," he laughed.

"I bet. I'm really surprised he hasn't been bothering us more about it. I'll go ahead and call him now before it slips my mind," Cookie said, rubbing Ken on the shoulder and giving him a kiss before picking up her phone to call her dad.

"Alright, babe. I'm cooking dinner tonight for you too. I should have everything ready in about an hour," he said. Meanwhile, he texted Charles. "Hey man, are you and the family available next Saturday? If so, bring your clothes and you all can spend the night here".

Charles texted back fairly quickly and said, "You bet. I know Lance and Alicia will be so excited. I'll let them know tonight and we'll see you next Saturday."

"Awesome. Sounds great. See you then. 4:00 pm sound good?" Ken replied.

* * *

"That works! Thanks man," Ken responded. He exhaled deeply, put his feet up on the ottoman in front of him and turned the TV from the news to find something more lighthearted. He stopped on an old rerun of *Friends*.

****

Next Saturday came quicker than Charles, Lance and Alicia expected. However, Lance was all too thrilled to visit his godfather and Cookie. "Hey, is it time to go over to Ken's house yet? Maybe we should get there a little early," he urged.

"Or maybe you should just hold your horses, little man. Is that ok? Your dad and I are really excited about seeing Ken and Cookie too. But we have to take care of some things around the house first. We'll be there in about two hours or so. I promise we will be there soon enough. Mommy has to wash your uniforms for next week. You don't want to play in the game next week with a dirty uniform, do you?" Alicia smiled.

"Hmmmm, I guess you make a good point. Carry on then. I'll wait," he slumped on the couch, with his arms folded, starting up a game on his Xbox.

"Excuse me, mister. Carry on? That's no way to talk to your mother. We will get there soon enough knuckle head," Charles said, putting Lance in a playful headlock and rubbing his fist on the top of his head.

"Dad! I'm going to lose my game!" Lance laughed, as he unsuccessfully tried to squirm away from his dad's grip.

"Hey baby, is there anything else you need help with? All the trash is out and the dishes are put up. Lance's bag is packed too.

You might want to double check it, in case I forgot something," Charles said.

"Ok, I'll check it in a minute. I think that's it. We can let the clothes run in the dryer and be on our way. Can you believe Cookie is pregnant? I just still can't believe it. I am so happy for them. Maybe I'm crazy, but it almost feels like we're expecting too," she smiled.

"I can't say I share the exact same sentiment. I think this one keeps us on our toes enough. I agree that it is surreal though to know they are expecting a baby. Seeing them both as parents is going to be a riot," Charles laughed.

"True, it will be. I think they will be great parents," she said.

"Oh yeah, no doubt. I agree. They will be," Charles said.

Lance was so enthralled in his video game that he forgot about his anxiousness to see Ken and Cookie. He was totally oblivious that it was time to leave.

"Guess what, little big man?" Charles asked.

"Huh?" Lance replied, never looking up from the TV, furiously punching the buttons on the controller.

"It's time to go now. You can finish out this game, then let's get loaded up in the car," Charles informed him.

"Yeah! Ok cool. Only two more minutes and I'll be ready," Lance replied. All the while, his bright smile remained on his face.

Meanwhile, Cookie and Ken were at home finalizing everything they needed for their weekend guests. "I think we're all set. I have the meat for the turkey burgers and all of the vegetables, condiments; oh and the fries too," Ken said.

"Ok, sounds good. The guest rooms are ready upstairs. What about the wine and the cheesecake bites?" Cookie chimed in.

"Yep, got those too. Are you sure about the wine? I feel guilty that all of us will be drinking except you," Ken said.

"Well, I think we both want a healthy baby, so I will be just fine. No need to stop the party for everyone else. Lance and I will be just fine with our virgin sangrias. I'm so excited to have company. You know how much I love entertaining. I'm a little surprised you agreed to have them spend the night so quickly," Cookie said.

"Oh really? What makes you say that?" Ken asked, with a confused expression on his face.

"Well, out of the two of us, I know I'm always readier to have company over than you are," Cookie laughed.

"Alright. Ok, I guess you do have me there. That is true," he chuckled.

"I tell no lies man. It's 3:45 now. They should be here any minute," Cookie said, as she gave the non-alcoholic sangria one last swirl before placing the punch bowl in the refrigerator.

⊛ ⊛ ⊛

114

Chapter 13

"Come on! This doesn't make any sense. They should have opened the door by now," Lance said, standing on his tip toes, ringing the doorbell again.

"Lance, that's enough. I'm sure they heard the doorbell ring. They will be here in a moment," Alicia said, shaking her head and rolling her eyes sarcastically at Charles.

"Hey, that's not what big boys do. Big boys are patient and they have self-control. Remember?" Charles reminded his son.

"Yeah, I know. I'll be patient," Lance responded with his arms folded. Just then, the knob turned from the inside of the house. Ken opened the door and greet them all. He picked up Lance and acted as if he was going to toss him in the air.

"Now, either I'm getting old or you are growing mighty fast Lance! Goodness, you aren't as light as you used to be. I guess all those games are building up some muscle, huh?" Ken said.

"Yep, I'm pretty strong," Lance said, flexing his arms, trying to show off his muscles after Ken placed him back on the floor.

"Oh, he's just so modest, isn't he?" Alicia laughed.

"Nothing wrong with a little confidence. Come on in," Ken replied, giving Alicia and Charles both a hug.

"Man, it has been way too long since we've all gotten a chance to hang out. Truth be told, we were just as excited as Lance was, but we couldn't let him know that," Charles whispered to Ken, laughing.

● ● ●

"Cookie! Look at you. You are glowing! You look so beautiful pregnant," Alicia said, giving Cookie a tight squeeze.

"Aw, you are too kind Alicia. You are the one. Then again, you have always looked amazing. Charles is such a lucky man," Cookie smiled.

"Hey babe. Did you hear that? You better be counting your blessings," Alicia laughed, looking back at Charles. He and Ken were just making their way in from the living room, with Lance following closely behind.

"Oh I know I'm a lucky man. Why do you think I married you so quickly? I couldn't let another man walk away with all that," Charles laughed. "Cookie, it's so good to see you. Ken and Cookie, proud parents to be. If this isn't a Kodak moment, then I don't know what is."

"I know, right. Can you believe it? We are so excited and ready to find out the sex too," Cookie chimed in. Lance looked on patiently until finally his curiosity got the best of him.

"Is it safe to give you a hug? I'm pretty strong you know, and I don't want to hurt the baby," Lance boasted.

"Mmmm, let me see. I might need to stretch a bit first," Cookie said, playfully putting each of her arms behind her head. "Come on, show me some love. I think the baby can withstand it."

"Ok, if you say so," Lance said. He got a running start and wrapped his arms around Cookie's very pregnant stomach. He put his ear to her belly and listened intently.

"Lance, that's enough now. Let Cookie breathe," Alicia said.

* * *

"I could hear the baby moving around in there. That's so cool," Lance smiled wide. His eyes lit up at the thought of the life growing inside of Cookie.

"See what you and Ken have to look forward to?" Charles joked.

"Hey, we are down for the challenge," Ken said, smiling and kissing Cookie on the cheek.

"We decided we would have a grill night and I made a special drink for Lance and me to sip on. Don't worry. There's wine too. We have some chicken and ground turkey to throw on the grill to make burgers. The meat is already seasoned too. We have some fries and cheese sticks too, my new obsession," Cookie said.

"What? You too? Charles will tell you during the last trimester of my pregnancy, I was so hungry for cheese sticks. That is too funny," Alicia said.

"Dad! Can we play a quick round of catch while the food is cooking?" Lance asked.

"Not right now son. I'm going to help Ken grill the meat, but you can come hang out with us," Charles said.

"I tell you what. How about as soon as the meat is on the grill, we can play a quick round?" Ken added.

"Yeah! You rock Ken!" Lance jumped up and exclaimed.

"Oh does he now? See, godfathers have it so have easy. That boy is spoiled rotten, I'm telling you," Charles said.

"Live a little man. He's just an excited boy. I'll get the grill fired up. The meat is already seasoned. So, we'll have plenty of time," Ken said.

"Ok, I guess you have a point. How about I watch the grill and you and Lance play? I know you don't get a chance to see him much. Plus, he sees me all the time. I know he would love that," Charles said.

Meanwhile, the ladies were inside trading pregnancy stories and discussing nursery room designs. "Cookie, this is truly amazing. I know you and Ken have got to be so excited to start your own family," Alicia said.

"Yeah, we really are. I'm just so nervous. You know? I'm trying to stop overthinking everything, but I just really want to be a great mother," Cookie replied.

"What do you mean? You will be. You're already a great wife. Nobody's perfect. You can't plan out everything. If something doesn't measure up to your expectations, it's ok. You just dust yourself off and keep it moving," Alicia told her.

"Well, you and Charles have always seemed like you've had it so together. So, I take your word for it," Cookie said.

"I appreciate that, but it's a work in progress. Trust me, Charles and I are by no means perfect. We just always try to make the best decisions for our marriage and our family. We don't always do the best thing. Hell, you live and you learn," Alicia said.

"Then you get Luvs, right?" Cookie laughed, rubbing her belly.

"You are so silly, girl. But yes, then you get Luvs too," Alicia joked. They continued to converse with each other for the next half hour or so. Cookie always admired Alicia. They had similar personalities, which is likely the reason why they clicked so well. Finally, the men and Lance came through the kitchen door with delicious smelling meat from the grill.

"Hey, hey, hey. It's about that time," Ken said.

"Mmmm, I don't know if it's these hormones or I'm just starving but I could eat that straight off the pan. Let's get ready to dig in," Cookie said.

"Well, it was a joint effort. Ken already had the seasoning taken care of, so all I did was grill," Charles said.

"Sounds like it was a smooth process. I'll start toasting the buns. The table is already set. Ken, do you mind getting the drinks?" Cookie asked.

"Sure baby. Anything you need," Ken said, getting the wine glasses out to put on the table. He pulled the virgin sangria Cookie made from the refrigerator and onto the counter.

"Thank you, baby. Lance, when is your next game? We really need to make it out," Cookie asked.

"Yeah! You have to come see me play. I'm pretty good. My next game is this Thursday actually. At 6:30 pm. Will you be there?" Lance asked, his eyes wide with excitement.

"Ken, do you have anything going on Thursday evening? I can make sure I get off work in time to make it," Cookie said.

* * *

"Sounds like a plan to me. Let's make it happen," Ken agreed.

"I know you both are so busy. If you can't make it out, really, it's ok," Charles chimed in. His facial expression cautioned them not to make any promises they would fail to live up to.

"Nope. We will be there. I'd love to see my little man play," Ken said, smiling hard at Lance and then at Cookie. He was pleasantly surprised that she was even open to going to one of Lance's games. Then again, he shouldn't have been. That's the kind of woman she was.

"Whoa! This is going to be the best game ever. You, Cookie, Mom and Dad! I might need to get some extra practice in for the game," Lance exclaimed.

Alicia smiled and rubbed his shoulder. "If you can't tell, he's super excited. This will be great. I'm so glad we came over. We really needed to break up the monotony," she said.

"Of course, we're glad to have you over. Ken and I don't have much company, so we're excited for the opportunity to entertain. Let's dig in before the food gets cold. Babe, the wine should be chilled now. Do you mind pulling it out of the freezer?" Cookie asked Ken.

"Wine coming right up," he replied. Everyone started preparing their plates while Ken tended to the drinks.

"Oh, the fries! I almost forgot about those," Cookie said, right as the Alexa alarm sounded off. Thank goodness for timers. I hope you all don't mind, I baked them instead of frying them."

* * *

"We are not picky. We are just glad to be hanging out. Plus, these two love potatoes any way you serve them," Alicia laughed, looking over at Charles and Lance.

"Go ahead. Don't wait. Please, help yourselves," Ken insisted.

"Alright then, this looks and smells so great. Maybe we can grill at home more often then," Alicia nudged Chares.

"Yeah I'm not too shabby on the grill when I want to be," Charles said.

"Uh oh, don't let me cause any dissention in the home. Alicia, he just simply flipped the meat over on the grill. That's it," Ken let out a hearty laugh.

"I'm sure he did. Well, I must extend my compliments to both chefs. This burger is amazing. Lance must think so too. If he's quiet while he's eating, that's a good sign," Alicia said.

Lance responded with a smile and a thumbs up in between quick, devouring bites. Cookie's heart melted as she looked at Lance enjoying his food, while Charles and Alicia watched his every move. This was what family looked like. She was getting more and more excited to start her own family with Ken.

Chapter 14

"Good morning, babe. I'm sorry, I was trying to be quieter and not wake you up," Sheila said.

"Oh, you don't have to worry about that babe. I woke up on my own. The way you put it on me last night, I would have slept right through a tornado," Sean said, giving Sheila a mischievous grin.

"Well look who's talking sexy. You were putting in overtime on me last night. Hey, I'm not complaining though. I slept just like a baby myself," Sheila replied. Sean could see her quick, slightly frightened expression change in the mirror, from the bed.

"Hey baby, what's wrong? If I didn't know any better, I would think you just saw a ghost or something," Sean asked.

"I can't lie, that's how I've really been feeling lately. Does the house feel any different to you since we used that stuff I got from Cookie?" she asked him.

Sean got out of the bed now and walked over to the vanity to brush his teeth and get closer to Sheila to see her better as she was talking. "You know, it's funny you mention it. I actually thought it was a little worse, but I just didn't want to say anything."

"Are you serious? Thank goodness. I'm glad to know it's not just me. I thought I was going crazy," she said, with a sigh of relief and uneasiness. On one hand, she was glad that Sean could recognize the eerie presence in their home. However, she was bothered by the fact that they both still felt it and it seemed to be intensified.

● ● ●

"Yeah, a couple of times when I've come home lately and it's just me here, the door slams behind me before I even get a chance to close it," he confessed. He didn't want to open this can of worms with Sheila. She was already paranoid about what was going on in the house. He couldn't lie to her though. Furthermore, she would be able to tell the difference if he was.

"Really? I haven't had anything happen like that but sometimes when I'm walking around the house, I feel this gust of wind come behind me. It almost feels like there's a presence or person running behind me. This shit is really starting to creep me out. I know when we first used that dust, I didn't feel it anymore for about a week. Now, it's back full force and seemingly worse than before," she said, bringing her hands to her face.

"Maybe we used the dust wrong? As much as I hate to even tap into that stuff anymore than we already have, maybe we should ask Cookie if we did it the right way," he said. Sheila was honestly taken aback that he even suggested entertaining the voodoo again to get the evil spirits out of their house.

"Voodoo with an instruction manual; imagine that," Sheila laughed. "You make a really good point though. I'll give her a call today and double check to make sure we did it right."

"Yeah, it's worth a try at least. In the meantime, I need to get in touch with Ryan to give me the real deal on what he knows about this house. Maybe if we tell him what's been going on with us, he'll finally be honest and tell the whole truth," Ryan said.

"That sounds good. I'm really scared. I just want our home to happy and peaceful," Sheila said.

"I know baby. So do I. We'll figure this out. I won't have you feeling this. I'll get to the bottom of it," Sean said dialing Ryan's phone number. He waited as Sheila could hear the multiple rings before it eventually connected to his voicemail.

"Hmph. Let's see how long it takes his ass to call back this time," she whispered.

"Hey Ryan, this is Sean. Listen, I really need to talk to you about this house. We need to know if there's some more information about it that we should be aware of. Something strange is going on here. Call me back asap," Sean explained.

Meanwhile, Sheila texted Cookie to ask her if they could meet for lunch this week. She figured she may still be sleep, getting ready for work or already there. She didn't want to disturb her if she was busy, but she did give her friend a hint of the sense of urgency. "Hey girl, hope you and the little bundle of joy are doing good. We should meet for lunch this week. Let me know what day works for you. Need to talk," Sheila typed.

"You know what? When Cookie first got this magic dust crap, it came with a little not of instructions. It almost looked like a scroll. She said she couldn't find it, but I'm going to ask her again," Sheila said.

"We need those instructions. Hell isn't that what those big books are for in the scary movies? How to cast the perfect spell?" Sean asked.

He was serious, but Sheila couldn't help but laugh. "You have the most amazing way of making the most unsettling situations have a silver lining," she said, rubbing his shoulder.

● ● ●

"Well I'm glad to make you smile, even during a time like this baby. I'm going to hop in the shower and get ready for work babe," Sean said, kissing her on the cheek.

"Do you want me to make you a smoothie babe? I know you're probably a little crunched for time," Sheila said.

"See there. That's why I love you. Teamwork. Yes, if you don't mind baby that would be great. Thank you," Sean said.

"No problem. Smoothie coming right up. I love you too," Sheila said. She stood there in the vanity a little while longer, watching Sean step into the shower. She always loved his thick legs and his physique was quite a sight to see from behind. Well, who was she kidding? He was a knockout from any angle. She waited until he got all the way in the shower and then walked up to the curtain.

"You think you have a few extra minutes to spare before making the smoothie? This peach is juicy and it needs some tending to," she said, with a sexy grin on her face.

"Damn baby. Come on in. Let me give that peach some love," he replied, admiring her smooth skin and perky breasts as she stepped in to join him in the shower. He kissed her neck and then made his way up to her mouth, sucking on each one of her lips separately before slipping his tongue inside her. Sheila grabbed the back of his head with both hands and pressed her naked body firmly against him.

Sean backed up to the seat inside of the shower and Sheila turned her back towards him. She grabbed his ample extremity and placed it inside of her slippery, tight opening. He moaned loudly as he entered inside of her. Sheila let out a high-pitched sigh as

* * *

she pushed back in contrast to Sean's forceful movements. He grabbed both of her supple breasts in the palms of his hands and squeezed them for dear life. He kissed the back of her neck and moved his hands down to her waist, pushing her down on top of him even further.

Sheila bounced on Sean's lap harder and harder, the more he kissed her. He then wrapped his arms around her waist, turned her around (while still inside of her) and made her face him. He put her ankles up on his shoulders as she shuddered with intense pleasure. Sheila then started moving her hips in circular motions. She could feel Sean throbbing inside of her and she knew he was about to climax. He could feel it too and he never was able to last too long whenever she moved like that.

"Yes, baby! Don't stop! I'm cuming Daddy! Ahh!" she screamed, with her hands wrapped around his head, feet still resting on his shoulders. He put her feet down and wrapped her legs around his back as he began to thrust harder and faster. He quickly climaxed right after her. Sheila could feel all his love juices exploding inside of her and it made her tingle even more. At that very moment, she didn't give a damn who or what was haunting their house.

● ● ●

Chapter 15

Bill could hardly wait for the arrival of his new grandchild. Although there was a pang of sadness, he felt without Lisa there to witness it too, he could feel that she was there in spirit. Then there was Chelsea. His sweet girl. He never quite forgave himself for being unable to help her more. There had to be something he could have done to cure her addiction. He was a strong man, but he began to feel lonely in his older age.

However, he realized that an idle mind was the devil's workshop. So, he kept himself busy with various home improvement projects around the house. He wasn't as sharp as he used to be, but he was still extremely handy around the house. He decided the kitchen and bathroom floors needed a bit of a facelift. Bill stopped by a specialty hardware store that sold hard-to-find tile.

He walked in and made a B line to the back of the store where the tile was located. He noticed a younger woman, likely in her mid-40s, perusing down the aisles. After the second time he spotted her, he had an eerie feeling that she may be following him. He just brushed it off and chalked it up to harmless paranoia.

That's when he found it. The beige and pearl colored tile he was looking for. He had a flashback of Lisa telling him that he needed to sit down and smell the roses. "Bill, you couldn't relax if your life depended on it," she would say. They would both laugh. His usual response was, "I don't know about that. I know how to relax". She was totally right. Nevertheless, he needed this to help ease his mind. Besides he was sure Lisa would be proud of him. Chelsea would too.

"Sir, I'm open here in lane 3," the cashier said, delicately trying to get Bill's attention.

"Oh, I'm sorry mam. I guess I was in a daze in my own world there," Bill said, as he watched the woman in the store walk outside the double sliding doors that were right in front of him.

"Hey, it's quite alright. Trust me, I do it all the time. This is such a beautiful color. Doing a little bit of remodeling at home?" the cashier asked.

"Yes, in fact I am. I've always been a DIY kind of guy before the kids started using that term. No one else will put the same special attention to it like you can," he replied.

"Well, amen to that. I tell people all the time that YouTube can teach you how to do anything. I may not be as strong as most men, but I'm pretty handy for a lady, if I do say so myself," she said.

"Hey, well there's nothing wrong with that. In fact, it's admirable. Well, you enjoy the rest of your day. It was great chatting with you," Bill said.

"Alright sir. You enjoy the rest of your day too and hope the project goes well for you. See you soon," the cashier said, flashing a bright smile.

Bill looked around the parking lot as he walked to his SUV to load the tile he purchased. The day was beautiful, so he slowed his pace slower than usual to soak up the sun. "Mr. Brighton?" a female voice uttered sternly. Bill guessed from the proximity of the sound, she was literally right behind him.

* * *

"Yes, I'm Mr. Brighton. You are? I'm sorry. I don't think I've had the pleasure of meeting you before," Bill said, turning around to face the woman, with the rest of the tile still sitting in the basket.

"Yes, how rude of me. My name is Sasha Primpton. I'm with the Chicago PD," she paused, letting him catch his guard. Although, she was surprised that he remained perfectly calm and collected. After all, it's not every day that someone gets stopped by the police for questioning.

"Chicago PD? Ok, well young lady, I'm not sure what you need from me, but how can I be of assistance to you?" Bill asked, with a cool demeanor, looking Sasha square in her eyes.

"Yes, it's a beautiful day out here today. I don't want to delay you from enjoying it. Mr. Brighton, you knew Mr. James Caldwell, right?" she asked.

"Yes, of course. He was a close friend of mine," Bill replied.

"Ok, well I know he has been deceased for quite some time now. I'm sorry for your loss. I know it was a devastation for many people, including his wife. Do you recall where you were the night of his death?" she asked.

"Yes, I remember it like it was yesterday. That was a hard week. My daughter had just been released from the hospital. She struggled with drug addiction. I was at home that night with my daughters and my wife," Bill said, fighting back tears thinking about Lisa and Chelsea being gone.

"Ah ok, I see. We recently received an anonymous tip from someone who said they briefly saw a black Lexus SUV parked in front of the Caldwell's home that evening. Are you sure you

• • •

didn't stop by to see him, even for a few minutes, that evening?" she inquired again.

"I'm positive. If you don't mind, I really need to get back to my day. Are there any other questions you have for me?" Bill asked.

"No sir, you're free to go. Thank you for your cooperation. Here's my card. Give me a shout if you think of any other information you would like to share. This case is still open and we would like to put this one to bed," Sasha said.

"Alright then and by the way, many people have a black Lexus SUV. I don't get how that relates to me, but I'm sure you're just doing your job. Can't be too careful, I guess," Bill replied.

"Yes sir, that is very true. That's what I'm paid to do. Oh, I do just have one more question, though. Do you know any reason why Mr. Caldwell would have any enemies? He seemed like such a loving and caring man. It's hard to believe that he would have met his demise in this way," she asked.

"He didn't have any enemies that I knew of. Everyone loved him. Then again, even Jesus had enemies. Guess that brings you back to square one then, right? You have yourself a lovely day, Ms. Primpton," Bill said, loading the rest of his tile in the vehicle.

"Point taken. Enjoy your day. Don't forget to call me with any information you have," she said, walking back to her car. Sasha sat in the parking lot and watched Bill pack up the rest of his tile and calmly drive away. He didn't seem the least bit bothered or afraid. However, she was aware of Rev. Caldwell's dark past of assaulting young girls. After all, she should know because she was one of them. To this day, no one knew what he did to her. She

* * *

secretly wished she would have been the one to kill him. She just didn't have the guts to do it. Sasha didn't know much about Mr. Brighton, but she figured he would have killed Rev. Caldwell if one of his girls was harmed. If that was the case, he didn't know that she would congratulate him for taking out the man she held a seething hatred in her heart for.

Chapter 16

"Hello? Hey Chelsea. How are you baby?" Bill said. He had just placed the last stack of tile in the garage before he went inside the house.

"Daddy? Are you ok? It's me, Cookie," Cookie replied, feeling a huge lump forming at the back of her throat. She thought about her sister every day, but this was the first time in a while she heard her name spoken aloud.

"Hey Cookie. I'm so sorry. I just…..it's been a bit of a rough morning. That's all," Bill said.

"What do you mean? Talk to me. What happened?" Cookie asked, with a very concerned tone in her voice.

"Let's just say karma may be catching up to me. This lady, her name was Sasha Primpton. She's with the Chicago police department. She followed me in the store today. I could tell something was up. Long story short, she started questioning me about Caldwell's murder," he paused.

"Wait. Say no more. I get it. You're ok though, right?" Cookie was paranoid that his phone may now be tapped. She didn't want her father to do anything to incriminate herself.

"You're right. We can finish it up when we see each other in person. I guess it just kind of shook me for a bit. On to better things. How are you feeling? My grandchild will be here in less than 2 months. I simply can't wait," Bill said.

● ● ●

"Well, I'm doing great. Ken and I are very excited. But, I'm glad you told me about what happened with you too. I'm even more grateful that everything is okay. You know, Ken and I were talking about you coming down here right before the baby is born. We thought it would be great to have you here," Cookie said.

"Really? That would be amazing. I would be honored. Just let me know when and I'll catch a flight there," Bill said, with excitement filling his voice.

"It will be great. The baby will be here before we know it. We'll pay for your plane ticket too, so don't worry about that," Cookie said.

"Well, thank you. I appreciate that. How about I make a crib for the baby while I'm there? That is if you all don't already have one. I know you move quickly," he laughed.

"Hmmm, you are actually in luck. We don't have a crib yet. We were going to pick one out this weekend. We'll wait now. Yours will be much better anyway," Cookie responded.

"Great. I know just the type of wood to get too. I can't wait for it. Nonetheless, I'm being rude. You called me and I just started rambling," Bill said.

"No, that's ok. You are not rambling. I just called to hear your voice. I'm on my way back from lunch now. I wanted to get out of the office for a bit and get some fresh air. It's a beautiful day in Dallas today. We don't get this type of weather here too often, so I thought I would take advantage of it," Cookie said.

"That's much better than it is here. I've come to like the snow. As long as the sun is out, it lifts my spirits a bit. I could use a bit of that these days. But, please know that I am so very happy for you and Ken. I'll be seeing you soon. In the meantime, I'll be creating the design in my head for the new crib. I love you, sweetie. You take care and don't push yourself too much. Take it easy a bit," Bill ordered his daughter.

"Thank you, Daddy. Do you think you can save some of that advice for yourself too?" Cookie replied.

"I'll try my best. You're the one carrying another life. I'm just a stubborn man looking after myself," Bill laughed.

"Ok, I guess you make a good point then. I'll take your word for it. I love you too, Daddy." Cookie answered. Cookie smiled as she hung up the phone. Although the pain of her mother and sister's death still stung every day, she at least found comfort in knowing her father was still there. She was about five minutes away from her job. Cookie stopped at the red light when her phone rang. It was Sheila.

Cookie didn't have much time to talk, but she realized she hadn't responded to her friend's text all morning. She thought she should answer the phone in case it was something urgent. "Hello? Sheila, I am so sorry. I got your text earlier. I've just been so on the go this morning. I just got back from lunch. I talked to my dad the whole time," Cookie stopped to catch her breath.

"Don't worry about it. I hate to even bother you. I know you're busy. I just really need your help," Sheila said.

"Sheila, what's wrong? That dust is fool proof. Don't tell me you're still having those spirits or whatever was going on in your house?" Cookie replied. Her tone was playful at first, until she detected the authentic sound of fear in her friend's voice.

"Cookie, something really strange is going on in this house. I know this sounds crazy, but were you ever able to find those instructions for that voodoo dust? Maybe I did something wrong. I don't get it. I'm starting to see some crazy things. It's not just me. Sean notices it too. Then, there's her face. I keep seeing her face. I don't understand why all of this is happening," Sheila cried.

Cookie listened to her friend intently before uttering her response. She was mentally and emotionally exhausted, but she had to find the energy to be there for Sheila. She could tell she was in desperate need of a listening ear. "I lined the doorstep and the back door outside. I put some on all the windowsills. Isn't that the same thing you did?" Sheila asked nervously.

"Yeah. I mean, I'm sure it is. It has to be the same way I did it. I brought that gray purse with me that night. I don't even remember reading those instructions all the way through, but I'll look for it as soon as I get home tonight. I promise," Cookie assured her.

"This is so crazy. Maybe we should have just listened to Ryan after all and not even pursued trying to close the deal on this house. There's got to be more history that happened here than he's letting on to," Sheila said.

"Who knows. Maybe so. It is strange that he wasn't like the typical realtor just trying to get you into a shiny new house. I don't understand it either. We'll get those crazy ass spirits out of your house girl," Cookie said.

• • •

"Thanks for being such a great friend to me Cookie. I love you. How is my little nephew or niece doing? I know you think it will be a boy, but I agree with Ken. I think it's going to be a girl. I can just feel it," Sheila said.

"You have a 50% chance of proving either one of us wrong. You just might be right. I still think it's going to be a boy. The baby is good, moving around like crazy. I know this baby will have no patience. It's moving around so much, I think it's doing a dance routine in there. Thank you for asking though. I love you too," Cookie responded.

"Well, I know you are a busy working woman for two now. I'll let you get back to it. Hey, don't forget to find those instructions. I'm a mess. I never thought I would be begging to find some voodoo instructions to ward off evil spirits," Sheila joked, with a slightly serious tone.

"Now, do you believe?" Cookie inquired in a spooky voice. "I'm just playing. I will try to find the instructions tonight. I'm sure you did it just like you were supposed to. I'm sorry I didn't think to look harder to have the instructions for you before. I'm telling you, this pregnancy brain is really taking me out," Cookie laughed.

"Hey, you better enjoy that now. Pretty soon, you'll be complaining about not getting enough sleep at night. I am beyond excited. I truly cannot wait to meet my nephew," Sheila said.

"Ooh, you are a mess. You won't know what to do with yourself if it ends up being a girl. That's alright though. When Ken and I can't get any rest, then we will bring him or her over to their godmother Sheila and Uncle Sean's. Well, that's after we clear those spirits out. Can't have my baby needing an exorcism," Cookie said.

"Ugh, bye girl. You are a complete fool," Sheila laughed heartily.

"Talk to you later," Cookie laughed back at her friend. She moved her car from the side of the street and pulled into the parking garage. She leaned her head back as she drove around slowly for a parking spot. Suddenly, she felt a wave of nausea and dizziness overtake her. This couldn't be. She had not vomited in weeks. She closed her eyes for just a second, hoping that would somehow take the feeling away.

When Cookie opened her eyes, she slammed on her breaks. She was about to hit a woman who was walking across the parking lot. She felt so careless and reckless, but grateful that she did not hit the woman. Then, she got a good look at her face. It was Chelsea. Cookie kept staring in disbelief at the woman who looked identically like her sister. She rolled her window down and put her car in reverse. She could see the woman's shoulders tensing as she put her car in her reverse.

"Lady, you should really be more careful. What were you thinking? You could have hit me!" the lady said, obviously frazzled and upset with the near brush she had with Cookie's car.

"Hey, I'm so sorry. I'm just not myself today. Please forgive me. It's just that you look like someone I know. That just really caught me off guard. I'm so very sorry. Here, it's not much but please have lunch on me," Cookie said, holding out a $20 bill out of the window. Now, that she got a closer look at the woman's face, she

● ● ●

141

could clearly see that she looked nothing like Chelsea. How in the world could she have seen her face so vividly?

"I don't need your money, but thank you. I have to get going now," the woman replied and walked off briskly.

Cookie would have put a wager on that woman being her sister. However, she couldn't fathom how the woman she almost hit with her car lacked a true resemblance to Chelsea. Although she blamed everything on her pregnancy hormones lately, this seemed different. Cookie exhaled deeply as she finally parked her car, trying to dismiss any thoughts that her mind was playing tricks on her.

Chapter 17

"Ah, goodness! I do not have time for this. I swear if I didn't love this girl...." Cookie said, as her voice trailed. Ken hurried into the bedroom and saw Cookie sitting on the closet floor, shuffling through several of her handbags and purses.

"Um, baby is everything ok down there? Do you feel alright?" Ken asked.

"Whew, you scared me baby. I'm good, just down here trying to find the instructions for that voodoo dust I gave to Sheila. They're still having issues at their house," Cookie answered.

"Wait a minute. I thought that stuff took out all the bad spirits. It seemed to work for us. They're still having ghosts in their house?" he asked.

"I don't know if it's ghosts, but there's definitely something wrong in that house. Sheila seems to think that she applied the dust the wrong way in the house and that's why the spirits are still there," Cookie said.

"All of this seems so confusing to me. Who knew that there was a science to it all?" Ken said, laughing and putting his work bag on the bed.

"You know, I actually thought the same thing too when I first started talking to her about it today. The more I listened though, I realized she's really scared. Hell, even Sean seems to be shook by it. That's how I knew it must be serious," Cookie said.

"I'm guessing you haven't found any luck yet with instructions. Do you remember how they look?" Ken asked.

"Yeah, they were on a little gray piece of paper. Goodness, I've been in this closet for about an hour looking for this piece of paper. Sheila has already called me too. I'm sure she wants to know if I've found it already," Cookie said.

"Wait a minute. Move your foot a little to your left baby," Ken said.

"Are you trying to play a trick on me. You are so silly," Cookie said, moving her leg as Ken instructed. She gasped when she saw what was right under her foot. The instruction sheet.

"Maybe it just took me to come in with a bird's eye view. Looks like that might be it to me," he said with a smile.

"I always knew you were my good luck charm. Wait, I am being so selfish right now," Cookie said, shifting the weight of her body to one side. She was attempting to get off the floor, but Ken didn't let her struggle.

"Here, give me your hands. I'll pull you up," Ken said, trying to prevent his wife from hurting herself.

"Sometimes I don't know what I did to deserve you. I was trying to stand up and give you a hug first. I didn't mean to just verbally vomit on you about Sheila's mess. How was your day, baby?" Cookie said, wrapping her arms around Ken's neck and kissing him passionately.

"Mmm, well after that kiss it doesn't even matter anymore. My day was pretty good. I'm just glad to be home now with my wife and my baby," Ken smiled, rubbing his hand on her stomach.

● ● ●

"That's the best news I've heard all day. Can you believe we'll get to meet this little person in just a few weeks? I love you so much baby," Cookie replied.

"I love you too, baby. I am so honored to have you as my wife and even more honored to have you as the mother of my child," Ken replied, kissing Cookie's very pregnant stomach.

"Hey, did you feel that? That was your Daddy giving you a kiss. You know, I'm starting to think that maybe you're right. We just might be having a girl," Cookie replied.

"Oh really? What makes you so sure?," Ken inquired.

"I don't know. Just seems like a feeling I've been having for the last couple of days. We shall see, literally. Anyway, I'll call Sheila now and read these instructions to her. If I don't, I know she will be blowing my phone up any minute," Cookie said.

"Alright then baby. Let me just put my clothes on and then get dinner started," Ken said.

Meanwhile, Cookie was patiently waiting for Sheila to pick up the phone. She had her Bluetooth on and was multi-tasking, trying to get her closet back in decent order again. Finally, Sheila answered.

"Hey girl, your ears must be burning. Sean literally just called me to ask if I had heard anything from you about the instructions. I told him I had to go because you were calling me. Can you believe Ryan still hasn't called or texted him back all day? I'm telling you, something about him just doesn't sit well with me. Just like this house. Ok, so please tell me I laid this stuff down the right way," Sheila asked, with a glimmer of hope in her voice.

"Let me see. I'm almost certain that you did. You know it's been a long time since I've even used this stuff. Ok, here's the first part. This is in all caps. It says, "LINE THE OUTSIDE OF YOUR DOOR WITH THE POWDER FIRST. LINING THE INSIDE FIRST KEEPS THE SPIRITS IN, NOT CASTS THEM OUT," Cookie said.

There was dead silence on the other end of the phone.

"Cookie. Um, I think I may have put it down wrong. I remember Sean asking me if I should start with the outside first and I told him he was wrong. I didn't listen Cookie. I didn't listen! Shit! Does this mean these crazy ass spirits will stay in our house? I can't take this. There's got to be something else that says otherwise," she said.

"I'm looking now. I'm so sorry Sheila. Dammit. I should have just found the instructions first when you initially asked for it. I just wasn't thinking clearly. I didn't think you would need them. Wait. There's another part here that directs you to line the inside of the house, just like you did. Then there's this other note right after that. It says, "If you've done any of these steps out of order, the problem can be fixed. However, you must return to the original person who sold you the product. These specific instructions must be followed accordingly, for the spirits to really be gone".

"Well isn't that great? So, I have to go see that crazy woman from New Orleans again? This is ridiculous. Will you come with me? Hell, if that's what it takes, then I have to meet her," Sheila said.

"Sheila, you know I would normally go with you in a heartbeat. I can't be down there and I'm about to have my baby," Cookie said.

* * *

147

"Please forgive me. This whole thing has really gotten my head in a haze. I'm sorry. I know you can't go with me. I don't even want you down there exposing my little nephew to all of that. Sean will go with me. I'll let him know tonight. Again, I'm so sorry Cookie for even asking you that. I'll let you go. Let me try to figure out when we can get down there," Sheila said.

"You know I'm ride or die. I just have to sit this one out. Plus, Ken would have a fit. Oh, wait. You said something earlier about seeing something. I can't quite remember what it was," Cookie inquired.

"Girl, there's no telling. I think I just probably misspoke. I love you sis. Thanks so much for looking. You have a good night, kiss Ken and rub your belly one time for me," Sheila laughed.

"Love you too. I will give Ken that kiss and I'm rubbing my belly right now. Bye," Cookie said.

"Alright then. I hear Sean pulling into the garage. I'll fill him in. Talk to you later," Sheila said.

"Wait! Wait. Sheila, I remember now. There was a face. A female's face that you said you keep seeing. Is it anybody that we know? Who is it?" Cookie asked.

Sheila got extremely quiet on the other end of the phone. The awkward silence lasted a few seconds too long. Cookie knew something strange was going on. Sheila couldn't lie to her friend now, but she had to protect her. Damn. She should have just shut her big mouth. "Face? You know all spirits have faces girl. Don't pay any attention to me. I haven't had much sleep lately. I'm probably just a little delirious. That's all," Sheila replied nervously.

"Sheila, I'm not there right now to look you in your eyes. I know you're lying to me though. Tell the truth. Come on now. What kind of face are you seeing at your house?" Cookie asked. Part of her didn't want to know, but she was too far gone now.

"Cookie, I'm so sorry. I really am not trying to bring any extra stress to your life right now. You know me like a book and I'm sure you won't let me slide with this one. The face I'm seeing is Chelsea's," Sheila said.

Cookie sat paralyzed in the moment. Sheila's voice seemed to have echoed for miles. She kept hearing her say Chelsea's name repeatedly. There had to be some truth to what her and Sean were seeing. Cookie saw it for herself earlier that day. The woman she almost hit originally had an uncanny resemblance to her sister. She dropped the phone from her lap and ran to the bathroom to vomit. Her emotions were swirling out of control and now, so were her insides.

● ● ●

Chapter 18

"Hey baby, I'm ready for the game tonight. I'll be off work by 4:00 today. Let me know if you need me to pick up anything on the way home," Cookie texted Ken, at 1:15 pm. However, Ken didn't see the text message until a few minutes after 3:00pm. He was so grateful Cookie reminded him. He felt horrible because he completely forgot Lance's game was later that evening.

"Goodness, I don't know what I would do without you baby. I'm ashamed to say I forgot about his game tonight. I had a meeting at 3:30 in the office, but I'll have to reschedule it for tomorrow. You are a lifesaver. See you soon. I love you," Ken responded back to Cookie.

"No worries. I guess this baby has us both stressing out a bit. Love you too, baby. See you at home," Cookie said. Cookie had a couple of big to-do items to check off on her list before she left. Nonetheless, Felicia came in her office, sat down in the chair and immediately started talking.

"So how is the beautiful mom to be doing? Haven't talked to you in a few days, so just catching up with you. I know you're not over here actually working. Girl, you are about to drop this baby in what, T minus 30 something days. You should be coasting and relaxing right about now. Let me get knocked up. That's exactly what I'll be doing," Felicia laughed.

"You are such a mess. I always know who to go to if I need to get my priorities in order," Cookie laughed. Although she always enjoyed Felicia's brass style of humor, she didn't have much time for it right then. Felicia had always watched her back against some people going after her role though, so she always felt a need to remain loyal to her. She didn't ever want Felicia to feel like she was brushing her off. Thankfully, she finally caught the hint.

"Hey, that's what I'm here for. I just needed a little distraction from work and Jerry. Can you believe he keeps trying to ask me out? Uh no. No way. I've tried to let him down subtly, but he doesn't get it. Cookie, his teeth are so crooked. Plus, he smells like Old Spice and nutmeg every day. In what world is that sexy?" Felicia exhaled, waiting for Cookie's response.

"Wait, not Old Spice and nutmeg. What decade is he living in?" Cookie pushed back from her desk as she laughed with Felicia. "You never cease to crack me up. Let me know if you need me to run any interference for him to catch the hint," Cookie said.

"Would you please? Pretty please, with a cherry on top and your first shot of rum when you can start drinking again?" Renita replied with her hands clasped together as if she was praying.

"Girl, stop before you make me pee on myself. You know my bladder is about as weak as his game is right now," Cookie laughed.

"Whew, I'll take that as a yes. Thank you. I owe you Cookie. Hey, what are your lunch plans for tomorrow? I have been dying to try out that new bistro that opened up the street from here," Renita asked.

"Oh yeah. I think it's called Breadbreakers or something like that? Sure, I would love to go. You make a good point. I feel like my head has just been down and I've been going nonstop these last couple of weeks. I could use a good break. Let me double check my calendar. Are you free at 11:45 tomorrow? I have a 1:30 that I can't miss".

"Let me see," Renita said, pulling out her phone. "Yep, let's do it. 11:45 it is. I'm free as a bird. Well, I'll let you get back to it. Hopefully, God has heard my cry and Jerry is nowhere near my desk when I get back. See you tomorrow," she said.

"Alright. I'm putting it on both of our calendars now, so we don't forget," Cookie said.

"Oh, you know I won't forget. But thank you. You always have been so on top of it with organization. I need to take a page from your book," Renita responded.

Cookie looked at the clock on her screen when Renita walked out of her office. 3:43 pm. There went her productivity. At least there was still a little time to start on the items she had on her check list. She would just need to come in a little earlier tomorrow to get the rest done. 4:00 came at lightning speed and before she knew it, it was time to pack up and head home.

Cookie barely sat her purse down in the passenger seat of the car before her phone rang. She assumed it was Ken, but it wasn't his ringtone. She immediately wondered who else it could be. Either her dad or Sheila. To her surprise, it was Alicia calling.

"Well, hello there. I am literally pulling out of my parking garage at work and heading to meet Ken at home. We can't wait to see Lance's game tonight," Cookie said as soon as she answered. There was complete silence on the other end of the line. Cookie pulled her phone away and looked at her bars. Surprisingly she had full service, even in the garage. She quickly pulled out next to the curb on the street but still didn't hear anything. "Hey Alicia. Are you there? Can you hear me?" Cookie asked.

"Cookie, um you and Ken don't worry about coming tonight," Alicia said with a cracked voice. Cookie could tell she had been crying.

"Hey, what's wrong? Talk to me. Is everything ok with Lance? What happened?" Cookie asked. She decided to stop asking so many questions and just let Alicia speak. She pulled into a nearby parking lot so she could freely talk to her without driving.

"Lance. He passed out at practice. Everything happened so quickly. He didn't say he was hurting. He seemed like everything was fine. But um, his speech started slurring and that's when he passed out. I called you first. Please relay the message to Ken. I gotta get back now. We just got here to the hospital, but I'll keep you posted," she said.

"Wait. Do you mind telling me what hospital you're at? Ken and I will just come there instead. I'll call him since he's probably just leaving work now too," Cookie said.

"Yeah, sure. Thanks so much. We're at the First Presbyterian Children's Hospital. I'll see you both soon then," Alicia said.

"Ok, thank you. Love you and we'll see you soon," Cookie replied.

She immediately dialed Ken to fill him in on the news. He picked up on the first ring. "Hey baby, I'm making my way home as soon as I can. Do you need anything? I can pick you up one of those teas you like," he said in an excited tone.

● ● ●

Cookie hated to burst his bubble, but she had to tell him what was going on. "Thank you, baby. But that's ok. We won't be able to go to the game tonight after all. Lance is sick and he's at the First Presbyterian Children's Hospital right now," Cookie said.

"Whoa. He's sick? What happened to him? I mean, it must be something kind of major if he's in the hospital, right?" he asked nervously. Cookie was taken aback by Ken's flustered response. Maybe she was just over thinking it.

"He's ok. I think he'll be fine. Alicia called me right as I was leaving work. I just hung up with her. She told me that his speech started to slur while he was at practice for the game. He passed out right after that. They aren't sure what caused it yet, but they're at the hospital. I just told her that we would come there instead. Do you want to meet at home first and then drive there together, since it's all on the way?" Cookie asked.

"Yeah baby. That works for me. Goodness, I wasn't expecting to hear this. I hope the little man is ok," Ken said.

"Me too. He's such a little fighter, I'm sure he will push through whatever it is," Cookie replied.

"Yeah, you're right. Listen, I'll see you at home shortly then babe. I love you," Ken said.

"Oh ok, I love you too. See you at home," Cookie replied. She tried to check her emotions at the door, but she couldn't help but feel uneasy about Ken's response. He was always so calm and put together. Maybe he had a rough day at work too. Something just didn't feel right. Cookie couldn't put her finger on it though. She was nervous to hear about Lance too, but she also had faith that he would be just fine. Nothing could get that little boy down.

She felt a sharp kick in her stomach as she pulled up to the red light, less than 10 minutes from home. She and Ken both loved that their jobs were relatively close to home, even in bad traffic. "Whoa now, that one kind of hurt mom a little bit. What are you doing in there? Huh?" Cookie said, smiling and rubbing her belly. She stopped to think about how Alicia must feel right now as a mother. Lance had no prior health problems that she knew of, so it must have been difficult for her and Charles. She said a prayer for their strength and for Lance's speedy diagnosis; more importantly his recovery.

Cookie was surprised to see Ken's SUV in the driveway when she pulled up. She assumed that she would end up beating him home. She immediately parked her car, grabbed her things from the passenger side and got out to greet him. He opened his door at the same time. Cookie could see the flushed look on his face as soon as she laid eyes on him. He was noticeably uneasy.

"Hey, I know we need to hurry. I'll get inside and change into something more comfortable and then we can be on the way," Cookie said, kissing Ken before walking towards the front door.

"You don't have to rush baby. I love you. I think I may change clothes too," Ken said, kissing Cookie back on the cheek.

"Why did he just kiss her on the cheek and not the lips?" Cookie thought. She hoped her breath didn't stink. Nonetheless, she felt as if her suspicions of Ken's frazzled state were confirmed even more now that she was standing face to face with him. They both quickly got dressed and jumped back in Ken's car to head to the hospital.

"They're at First Presbyterian, right?" Ken asked, as he started backing out of the driveway.

"Yes, that's the one. Here, I grabbed an apple for you. I know we don't have time to eat but wanted you to have something," Cookie replied, handing him the apple nervously.

"Oh no baby. You take that. Did you get to eat anything?" Ken asked Cookie.

"I ate a late lunch so I'm not that hungry. Plus, my stomach feels a little uneasy so I probably shouldn't eat anything right now. You take it and enjoy babe," Cookie replied, looking out the passenger window.

"Ok, I hope that queasiness goes away for you," Ken said, placing his right hand on Cookie's leg as he continued driving. He took the apple from her and began to eat it.

"It's ok. You know it comes with the territory," Cookie replied. She felt herself becoming a whiny brat and decided to just remain quiet the rest of the ride to the hospital. Ken was a good man and he never gave her any reason to question his loyalty and love. The one time he did couldn't even fully be counted.

Ken and Cookie walked inside the hospital and quickly looked for Lance. The receptionist directed them to room 306, where Lance was. Ken knocked on the door and Charles immediately opened it. "Oh my God. Thank you both for coming. Our little trooper got exhausted and looks like he's recovering just fine. They brought him back to give him some fluids," Charles said.

• • •

Cookie had to fight back her nagging thoughts again, as Charles didn't seem too worried about Lance. Even Alicia's demeanor was much calmer than when Cookie spoke with her on the phone. Nonetheless, Ken was entitled to handle things in his own way.

"Well, did the doctor say what was wrong? I'm so glad he's doing better. This may be the first time since he was a baby that I've seen him still and sleeping like this. He's such a ball of energy," Cookie replied, smiling down at Lance. He was sound asleep and looked well, minus the slight flushed tone of his cheeks.

"They basically said he just suffered from extreme exhaustion. They don't foresee it being anything major. Just sounds like that ball of energy finally came to a screeching halt. I think he will be ok though. They're just running some blood work too just to be on the safe side. He may get released tonight. I know he will be devastated once he realizes he didn't get to play at the game today. We really appreciate you and Ken coming out here," Alicia smiled.

"Of course, we had to come see about the little guy," Ken responded, gently grabbing Lance's hand. "I'm sure there will be plenty more games. We will make it a point to be at the next one".

"We will probably have to keep a close eye on him to make sure he doesn't stand in the way of his own health. That will no doubt be a hard task for Alicia and I," Charles laughed.

"Yeah he will bounce back in no time. I'm sure of it," Ken smiled. "Did they say when the blood tests should come back?"

Cookie shot Ken a bit of a scolding stare. Everyone was just on a happy note and giving positive affirmations about Lance's condition. However, Ken quickly brought everyone back down to reality. His question was valid and Cookie thought the same thing herself. That just wasn't the right time to bring it up.

"Um, well I think the tests will be back in a couple of days. He'll be ok, we're sure of it," Charles answered. Cookie could see the skepticism in his eyes.

Chapter 19

Cookie awoke the next morning with a slight headache. She attributed part of it to her lingering uneasy feelings about Ken and Lance's hospital visit. Now, she had swept his initial reaction under the rug. She knew if she were in Alicia's shoes, she wouldn't want to be reminded of potentially life changing news about her son at that moment. Maybe that was why men weren't made to be mothers. After all, she did always respect and appreciate his quiet strength, as awkward as it may have been at times.

She rolled over in the bed and found that Ken was already up. She could hear movement in the house but didn't know when he got out of bed. Cookie knew she must have been sleeping hard. Ken always joked about how he could never tip toe out of bed without her knowing. She generally slept as light as a feather.

"Hey there, sleeping beauty. You were knocked out as soon as you got in the bed last night. You looked so beautiful sleeping. I didn't even mind that you were snoring," he grinned, walking out of the bathroom naked, drying off from the shower.

"Damn," Cookie thought to herself. She heard his words on a delayed playback. His nude body standing there still dripping from the shower completely broke her concentration. She had something to look forward to after giving birth. Cookie couldn't wait to get another piece of him again. Wait a minute. "Did he just say I was snoring?" she thought.

"Um, I do not snore. You know that. You're just playing with me. Such a prankster," she laughed.

● ● ●

"Alright, don't believe me. Ask the baby. Did you hear Momma snoring? Yeah," Ken said, in a playful baby voice.

"Goodness, you're serious. I really was snoring. Oh wow, I am so sorry. I must have been more tired than I thought. I don't know what I'm still doing laying in this bed. I need to get up and start getting ready myself," Cookie replied.

"You don't have to apologize. After last night, for all I know I could have been snoring too. Feels like I slept really hard," he said.

"I think we both deserved a good night's sleep. I'm supposed to have lunch with Renita today. That girl is so crazy, but she keeps me laughing. I know there's probably some juicy gossip she wants to share. That's usually what going out for lunch means for her," Cookie laughed.

"Yeah, she is definitely on the spicy side to say the least. She has no filter at all," Ken said, starting to brush his teeth at the sink.

"When I drop this baby, I am tearing you up boy," Cookie said, grazing her nails across his back as she walked by to also get in the shower and start getting ready for work.

"You won't have to say a word. I'll be so ready for that," he smiled seductively back at her.

"Alright, we will see. Don't get ready. Stay ready," she grinned, as she stepped into the shower.

"Will do. Hey babe, I have a little time to make a smoothie this morning. How are you feeling? Do you think you'll be ok to have one?" Ken asked.

⚉ ⚉ ⚉

"Ah, yes that would be great, if you don't mind. Do you mind leaving the bananas out of mine this time? I think they made me nauseous," Cookie replied.

"Ok, one smoothie without banana coming right up," Ken said.

Cookie exhaled deeply and stared down at the precious life growing inside of her womb. She couldn't be more excited and prouder to be carrying Ken's baby. He was such an awesome husband. She knew he couldn't help but be an amazing dad as well.

"Hey babe, I'm about to finish getting dressed and then I'm about to head out for work. I left your smoothie in the refrigerator," Ken said, walking into the bathroom to give Cookie a kiss.

"Thank you so much. I'm sure it will be delicious. Have a great day baby if you're not here when I get out," she said.

"Same to you my love. See you tonight," he said.

Cookie remained in the shower for another 10 minutes or so. The water felt like a mini massage on her skin and she soaked up every minute of it. After she finished luxuriating, she stepped outside of the shower and heard her phone make an alert message. She dried herself off as she picked up the phone.

"Hey, it's me. Just reaching out. I know you're expecting soon. You're going to be a great mother Candy. We should catch up soon." Cookie felt as if her life was just one major surprise after another. The message in her Facebook inbox was from Mike. She hadn't had a real conversation with him since she was still married to Brandon. She always considered him a good friend, but she kept her distance with him after their last encounter.

* * *

Damn social media. She shouldn't have been so surprised that he reached out. Cookie told herself that it was just a nice gesture from an old friend. However, she couldn't bring herself to respond to him right now. She found herself getting anxious at the thought of him getting the read receipt from her looking at the text message. Oh well, he would have to know. Cookie decided it would just be best to respond to him later, when she was able to fully formulate what she should say.

Cookie's mind was racing for the entire duration of her drive to work. She kept envisioning how she would respond to Mike's message. She wondered why he decided to reach out now and if he had any ulterior motives. She hoped he didn't. Then, there was Sheila. She still hadn't fully processed that her best friend confessed that the spirit haunting her home could be that of her dead sister. The scary part was that Cookie didn't think it was so farfetched.

****

Meanwhile, at that exact moment, Sheila and Sean were less than two hours outside of New Orleans. They decided to make a road trip of it and use the time to clear their minds from everything going on. "Babe, we have to stop by one of those drive through daquiri shops. I think it's safe to say that we both deserve one after everything that's been going on," Sheila said.

"Yeah, you do make a good point. I could use a Hurricane right about now. Babe, I have a serious question to ask you," Sean said.

"Sure, what's that? Ask away," Sheila said, flailing her hand and making light of whatever he was about to ask.

"I'm not trying to be negative, I promise. Are you sure we are even going to run into this woman again? That was a while ago when you and Cookie were there. What if her store moved, or she doesn't want to tell us what to do, or she's dead?" Sean replied, anxiously rattling off his series of questions.

"Hmmm, I don't know. She's gotta be there though. You know those old voodoo people are the last ones standing, even after everything else is gone. We need this to get rid of whatever spirit this is. She'll be there. I'm sure she will. If she's not, then we will have to come up with a damn good plan B," Sheila responded, with a dazed stare, looking out the side of the passenger window as Sean drove.

"Goodness, those daquiris sound even better right now. Oh look, there's a sign right there. 20 miles ahead. Here we come. Hey, worst case scenario, I'm using this trip as a getaway with my beautiful, sexy and loving wife. I love you babe," Sean said, grabbing Sheila's hand and kissing it.

"I love you more. I'm so honored to be your wife and proud that you're my husband. You are truly one of the best things has happened to me," Sheila said.

"Umph, one of the best things, eh?" Sean said.

"You know what, you nut. Just make sure you don't pass up the daquiri shop, while you're trying to make fun of me," Sheila responded.

****

Cookie looked down at her watch. Thank goodness it was 10:15 am. Lunch with Renita was just around the corner. She decided she would text Mike back in the meantime, to help curb her thoughts of hunger. "Hey Mike, it's so great to hear from you. Yes, you heard right. I am going to be a mom soon. I hope all is well with you and Kelly? Let's catch up soon." Ugh, maybe she said too much. She leaned back in her chair and rubbed the back of her neck. Oh well. She didn't have the energy to overanalyze her response to him. She hoped he would just respond appropriately.

Before she knew it, Renita walked into her office to ask if she was ready to go to lunch. "Oh goodness. Where did the time go? I am so hungry too. I can't believe it's already 11:00 am. Let's get out of here. I am so hungry," Cookie exclaimed.

"Yes, I'm not eating for two but I damn sure feel like I am. Come on, let's go girl," Renita replied.

"Uh oh. Are you sure you don't have any news to share with me? Congratulations just may be in order," Cookie laughed.

"Grab those keys and let's go Cookie. Don't put that evil on me, Ricky Bobby. So wrong," she laughed back.

They walked swiftly towards the elevator to head downstairs for lunch. Just as the elevator door opened, Renita realized she left her cell phone at her desk at work. Renita's desk was located around the corner from Cookie's office. It wasn't exactly a far walk, but far enough for Cookie. She was starving and getting impatient. "I'm so sorry. I promise I'll be quick. Come on, walk with me if you don't mind," Renita said.

"How about I just stay here? You know I'll just be waddling down the hallway," Cookie sighed, with a tinge of agitation.

"Come on. Please. You know I need you to be my wing man against Jerry? I don't want to walk past him by myself," Renita.

"You better be lucky I like you," Cookie sighed and chuckled before catching her breath to walk with Renita.

"I won't be long. I promise. I know exactly where I left it," Renita said.

"Ok, I'm timing you," Cookie joked. They both walked around the corner, with Cookie striking up a frivolous conversation right before they walked past Jerry's desk. Renita's desk was a little further down the hallway. They passed her desk and Renita knocked on the office door on the back wall.

Cookie was seriously starting to get frustrated. Renita knew she was hungry and just appeared to be taking her sweet time. Maybe she was just irritable. Either way, her patience was paper thin.

Suddenly, the door swung open from the inside. There was a sea of pink and blue balloons floating at the top of the ceiling. There were colorful streamers hanging on the wall, a huge, decadent looking cake at the center of the table and Ken was sitting at the head chair. Renita had really pulled a fast one on her. Many people from the department were piled into the room. Cookie saw a spread of food along the back table. There were several beverages lined beside the food as well.

Tears began to stream down her face as Ken walked towards her to give her a warm, tight embrace. "I feel so loved. Ah, this is just amazing. I'm speechless. Renita, I'm really going to get you. How did you keep all this from me?" Cookie said, hugging Ken tightly.

* * *

"Well, if it makes you feel any better, I just found out a couple of days ago," Ken laughed.

All her coworkers took turns hugging her as Renita took the covering off the food she had catered for her. Cookie inhaled the aroma of the chicken wings and meatballs. She glanced underneath the table to see a row of various gift bags lined up for them.

"Alright everyone, we will let the beautiful mom to be and her husband get their plates first and then everyone else is free to dig in. Then we'll start with a little game. Don't worry Ken. I made sure not to make it too girly," Renita laughed.

"Ok, I prepared myself either way but I appreciate you looking out for me," he smiled back at Renita. Ken served Cookie's plate of food first before getting his own. She started sipping on the punch before she sat down. Cookie raved about how delicious it tasted. However, she was so hungry, almost anything sounded good.

Renita waited until everyone settled down before she explained the rules for the first game. "Ok, here are the rules to our first game. Everyone will get a sheet of paper entitled, "The Truth About My Parents". There are a mix of true/false questions about Cookie and Ken. The person who gets the most amount of answers correct wins the prize. Everybody got it?" she asked.

"Yes, I've got it! Let's play!" Marti exclaimed. No one in the office was extremely fond of Marti. She was excellent at her job, but she was far too sensitive for anyone's liking. Renita knew if she excluded her from the invitations, she would never hear the end of it.

* * *

167

Ken pulled his phone out of his pocket, since he kept feeling it vibrate. He opened the screen and saw he had two missed phone calls from Charles. There was also an unread text message from Charles that said, "Hey man, give me a call when you get a moment. It's about Lance".

Chapter 20

"Hey Charles. I called back as soon as I could man. Everything ok with Lance?" he asked. Ken didn't know what Charles had to tell him, so he thought it would be best to leave out the fact that he was just leaving the baby shower. He connected his Bluetooth on his ear as he slowed at the stop light after leaving Cookie's job.

"Thanks man. Hey listen. We got the blood work back from the doctor this morning. Lance is going to need a blood transfusion," Charles said solemnly.

"Ok, he's going to be ok though, right? I mean, what are the next steps to getting him a blood donor?" Ken asked nervously. He was trying to be strong for his friend, but it was nearly impossible for him to mask his concern.

"That's the thing. I would have given the blood myself, but my blood type isn't compatible with his. It's the weirdest thing. You would think I'd be able to give blood to my own kid. Alicia's anemic, so it's not a good idea for her to give blood either. Now we just have to wait," Charles said.

"What type of blood does he need?" Ken asked.

"The doctor was talking a mile a minute. I'd have to go back and ask Alicia. I know she took notes on all of it. I am sure that O positive was one of the ones he said. If we could find someone with that blood type, that would be perfect," Charles replied, with a defeated tone.

"Charles, um, I think I have the solution to the problem," Ken uttered.

⁕ ⁕ ⁕

"Really? I know my mind is a little hazy right now. I'm sure you're about to tell me something I've overlooked," he said.

"No, but my blood type is O positive. I'll give my blood," Ken said.

"Oh my God! Are you serious Ken? You would really do that for us? Wow, thank you so much. I'll tell Alicia tonight. We owe you big time," Charles exclaimed with glee. Ken could hear his immense excitement and relief over the phone.

"Of course, man. There's no way I could sit back and let Lance sit on one of those waiting lists when we can do it now. Keep me posted. I'll let Cookie know tonight too. I'm glad I can help," Ken said.

"Ok, that's good. Sounds like a plan. My boy is going to be alright. I love you man," Charles replied.

"Love you too Charles. Lance will be back to normal in no time," Ken responded.

"That's right. Well, I'll talk to you later man. I'll give you a call back as soon as I find out more information," Charles said.

Ken rummaged through his thoughts of fear, relief and pride. He was afraid about Lance's health condition. How bad had things really gotten? What else did the doctor say that he was unaware of? He hoped the blood transfusion would be the end of it. However, he was also thankful that it could have been worse. Lance sounded like he would be well on his way to a full recovery, with no side effects as soon as he got the blood transfusion. Ken was also glad that he could do more than just stand by and offer words of encouragement to Alicia and Charles. He could offer them something tangible to assist with Lance's well-being.

* * *

He decided to work from home for the rest of the day, since he wasn't too sure how long the baby shower would last. Ken packed the heavy gifts with him. There were so many, he had to put some in Cookie's car too. Cookie arrived about an hour after he got settled in at home. Ken immediately went to the garage to unload all the gifts. He could see she was still beaming with joy when she pulled in.

"Hey baby, I see you did decided to work the rest of the day from home. I'm so glad. Goodness, I hope I don't look a mess. I've been crying the rest of the day. I really didn't expect them to do all of that for us. Weren't you surprised too?"

"Yeah I haven't been here long though. Maybe an hour or so. You look beautiful baby. You don't look a mess at all. Don't you lift a finger. Just get comfortable and I'll get everything out of the car. I was really surprised at everything we got too," Ken replied. Honestly, he wasn't the least bit surprised. Cookie was so loved at her job that he didn't expect anything less. He didn't want to rock the boat and ruin her great mood though.

"So, how was the rest of your day? I know you said Charles reached out to you. Is everything still good with Lance? That little boy is such a fighter. He's so cute," Cookie smiled.

"Yeah, I did get to talk to him. Everything is good, but he's just going to need a blood transfusion pretty quickly," Ken replied.

"Oh wow, ok does he have a donor? What am I thinking, I'm sure Charles or Alicia can give the blood to him right?" Cookie inquired.

* * *

172

"Well, that's the thing. Alicia is too anemic to give blood and Charles's blood type isn't really the best match for it. He told me they really need O positive blood, which I have," Ken said.

"Ok, so what are you saying? Wait, are you thinking about giving the blood to him?" Cookie asked, with a concerned expression on her face.

"I actually just told Charles I would a little while ago. It just all happened so fast. He needs O positive blood, which is what I have. It just seemed like the right thing to do. Sorry I didn't get to talk to you about it first babe," Ken said, in a sincerely apologetic tone.

"Ken, that's a very noble thing that you agreed to do. I just really wish I would have been the first to know. When will you have to give the blood? The baby's almost here and I'm just afraid. I'm nervous lately and this just all seems so out of character for you. Maybe it's me. Maybe I'm just going crazy or something," Cookie said.

"Baby, I get that you wanted to know first. Believe me, I wanted to tell you first too. I really think you might be over reacting just a little bit though. If I didn't step up, Lance would be on a waiting list for God knows how long. I'd like to think that you would have done the same thing if you were in my shoes," Ken replied, now clearly agitated.

"Well, I'd like to think if you were in my shoes you would have thought first before making that kind of commitment. Goodness, I know he's our godson but you're acting like he's your kid. We have a baby of our own on the way and I can't do this alone. I got a few more gifts after you left. You may not have seen those, but it looks like you've already gotten everything out of the car. I'll just show them to you later. I'm about to go lay down for a bit," Cookie said dryly.

Ken started to walk after her to plead his case but decided it might be best to leave her alone for now. He didn't want to upset Cookie, but he was really shocked she took the news so negatively. He was only trying to help Lance. There was no way he could live with himself if Lance's conditioned worsened because he failed to help him.

There was nothing he could do about it now. He had to let the steam blow off and figure out a way to still help Lance, without offending Cookie. Ken just wasn't sure if that was even possible. He felt his phone vibrate in his pocket. He took it out and viewed an unread text message. It was from Alicia.

"Hey Ken, Charles told me about you volunteering to be a blood donor for Lance. I would call, but I am in tears. Can't even speak right now. Thank you, thank you, thank you. Please tell Cookie I said thank you too. We really appreciate it," Alicia said.

Ken stared at his screen before he responded. His fingers moved on auto pilot, as he replied to Alicia. "Of course, you're welcome! I'm sure you and Charles would do the same for us. We love Lance and we're happy to help him out in any way we can. Anytime."

Chapter 21

"Do you think it was this building?" Sean said, pointing down the damp sidewalk on Bourbon Street. The nightfall was already starting to set in. Once they reached the hotel, Sheila and Sean stopped at a Cajun seafood restaurant. They stayed long enough to eat and let their buzz wear off. Afterwards, they continued traveling down Bourbon street.

"No, it definitely wasn't a building like that. Too colorful. This lady is in an old wooden, gray looking building with fluorescent neon green lights on the outside. I'm telling you, it looks like a dump. Wait, let's keep walking down here. I think we're getting closer to it. I remember this strip club that wasn't too far down the way from it. It's ridiculous the things you don't realize you remember," she laughed.

"Hey, no judgment here," Sean chuckled.

"Um hmm, I'm sure. Don't get distracted mister. Besides, I can always give you a strip tease in the hotel room later," Sheila sneered seductively back at Sean.

"Well, let's just ditch the old lady and get back to the room then," Sean said.

"Babe, I need you to focus. Come on now. You know this is important. We have to find this old hag. We need her to reverse these damn heebie-jeebies," Sheila urged.

Sean nodded as they kept looking down the street for a ragged looking building that resembled Sheila's description. He was beginning to wonder if they were doing more harm than good by coming to find this woman. There was no talking Sheila out of it though. He hoped their trip would be worth it and they could get rid of these spirits once and for all.

"That's it! Babe, this is it. That grey abandoned looking building straight ahead. The lighting looks so dim in there though. I don't remember that. Let's see," Sheila said, beckoning for Sean to catch up. Her adrenaline was running strong and she quickly started walking ahead of him.

A frail, tall man that reeked of alcohol stumbled out of rickety glass door. "Aye, um, may I help you with something? It's not every day I get customers racing to get in here," the man laughed.

Sean looked up at the top of the door. There was a jagged metal sign that had the name "Gheauxsts" carved into it with lights shining down on it. This had to be a joke. The place looked like child's play inside; not anything that would remotely be strong enough to ward off any evil spirits.

"I'm sorry, I think I must be mistaken. This isn't the same store I remember. May I ask what you sell here?" Sheila asked.

"Oh sure, I can show you better than I can tell you," the man replied, with a sinister grin.

"I don't mean to be rude, but we're kind of on a time crunch. Is this the same place that does readings? Palm readings, with dust and bones. You know, that sort of mumbo jumbo," Sheila replied nervously.

"Well, you're close, but no cigar. I have a couple of novelty games here and some voodoo rituals. Are you afraid of the word? After

* * *

all, that's exactly what it is. You're definitely in the right town for that," the man replied.

"Ok, do you know what happened to the voodoo shop that used to be here? There was a lady who had stringy gray hair, an olive skin tone and a raspy voice. Do you know who I'm talking about? I need to find her," Sheila said.

"Ooh wee, chile. I'd say the two of you are in serious need of getting revenge or rid of something very evil. You won't find her here though, I'm afraid," he said, redirecting his gaze to Sean.

"Look man, just tell us where to find the lady. The building doesn't matter so much. We just need to find her," Sean said, in an agitated tone.

"You guys are really serious then. You didn't hear this from me, but I know exactly who you're speaking of. She got tired of the rent going up here, so she does her rituals from home now. She lives just a few minutes from here," he said.

"Oh great! Thank you so much. What street does she live on? Do you know her address by chance?" Sheila pleaded.

"Here's something that will help you on your way. Don't tell her that I sent you though. I don't need her casting any of that wicked shit my way. My life is already cursed as it is. Oh, I'm Brian, by the way. How rude of me not to introduce myself. And you are?" he asked, wobbling as he extended his hand for a handshake.

"I'm Lisa. This is my husband Brad. Listen, we have to go but it was really nice meeting you. Thank you so much for your help," Sheila said, turning to walk out the door. Sheila thought it was incredibly ironic that the guy's name was Brian. Nevertheless, she

● ● ●

had to shake off her eerie feeling about their new acquaintance and get back to the issue at hand.

"Yes, thank you. Have a good night Brian. We'll get going now," Sean added.

"Well I would be remised if I didn't at least warn you about the landmines you're about to cross. Be careful with that lady. Some say her dealings with all those spirits has taken over her mind; not to mention the minds of others she meets. There have been a few missing persons reports from people who were last seen in route to her home. But you're grown and can make your own decisions. Safe travels," Brian said, as he turned away quickly and stepped back inside the establishment.

Sheila and Sean quickly glanced at each other with a disturbed look, before walking back to their car at the hotel. "I can't believe this. Baby, is it just me or is this story getting stranger by the minute? I get that we were supposed to come here to find this woman. That man makes it sound like we're about to be casualties of an Unsolved Mysteries episode. All of this just seems too eerie for me," Sean said.

"Just trust me, please baby. She'll remember me. I know she will. We'll just go to the house, get the instructions we need and leave. Nothing more. Nothing less. I know this seems crazy. I really owe you big time for this," Sheila retorted.

Sean drove as Sheila navigated the directions towards the woman's house. They were silent most of the way there, except for an occasional confirmation of directions. "Goodness, this road is so dark. Who the hell would want to live back here?

According to the GPS, we're only seven minutes away," Sheila uttered.

"Perfect. It's the bayou Amityville horror house," Sean said, as he heard Siri announce their arrival a few minutes later.

"I hope she's home. It looks so dark in there. Let's park a little further out, closer to the street. I just don't want us to get too close to the house," Sheila said nervously.

"Good call. Don't get out yet. I'll come over and open your door," Sean replied.

Sheila could feel the grass brushing against her ankles as she stepped out of the car. The grass had to be about four inches high; just high enough to feel uneasy walking in the darkness. They walked cautiously up to the front door of the house. Sean realized there was no real driveway, just a trail of dirt that served as a break in the rough, unmanicured grass.

"Wait. Stop baby. Did you hear that?" Sean whispered.

"No, I don't hear anything. What is it?" Sheila whispered back. Then, she immediately felt something nudging her pants leg. Great. She could tell it was an animal of some kind, likely a dog. She just hoped it didn't try anything vicious.

"It's ok, baby. Just stay calm. Don't show your fear. We only have a little bit before we get to the front door. Just one step at a time," Sean uttered.

"Ok, alright. I'm taking it easy. I've had dogs before. I like dogs. I've never had one this damn big as a pet or brushing up against

* * *

my leg outside at night though. But it's ok. We're almost there, like you said," Sheila said.

They made it to the bottom step of the front door before the dog started barking. He walked with them the whole way to the front door, without a sound other than his paws stepping on the creaking wooden steps. Now, he seemed angry and restless. Sean cautiously placed his foot on the second step. The dog hopped to the top of the steps and faced them. They could see its face clearer now. There was a dim porch light on. The dog appeared to be a mutt mixed with a Rottweiler. Sean stepped back down on the grass, as not to further agitate the dog. Sheila was even more startled when she looked into its eyes. The dog had a hazy gaze, with piercing gray eyes. It almost acted as if it was warning them from going inside the house.

Suddenly, the wooden door flew open and Sheila recognized the woman's face immediately. She was so thankful they found the right house. Now, if they could only get past the evil, mangy looking dog. "What the hell are you doing on my property? I'm so sick of these damned trespassers. If the dog doesn't get you first, I have something in here that will see to it that both of you are erased. What do you want?" she asked in an agitated tone.

"Hello, you may not remember me. I believe your name is Lilly. My name is Sheila. My friend Cookie and I met you a few months ago. You were at the shop on Bourbon Street then. Look, my husband and I really need some help,"

"Chile, do you know how many full moons have rolled over since whenever that was? I guess you're looking to me to fix your troubles now. No one ever comes here unless they are trying to kill someone or prevent a spirit from killing them. So, which one are you here for? Oh and your husband seems a bit too quiet for my liking. What's the matter chile? Are you afraid I'll bite? Oh and the name is Ivy, not Lilly yea," Ivy responded.

"Ms. Ivy, I'm here to support my wife. I don't need to speak many words. Look, we just need some directions on some magic dust that she got from you. We think we may have missed a step," he said.

"Hmmm….boisterous, with a quiet strength. I like it. Magic dust? Really? Oh bless your little gullible hearts. It's more complicated than that. You two sound like a hopeless case but come on in out of this night air. Move it Joe!" Ivy replied, ushering the dog to move from the front door. Surprisingly, Joe quietly walked away and past them back down the steps.

"Thank you. Well, my friend bought some of the dust for herself, but I used some too after my husband and I moved into our new home. Seems like there are some type of spirits there that we can't shake loose," Sheila said.

"Follow me. Hang your coats at the hanger on the back of the door. Have a seat here in the kitchen. I just made some tea if you'd like some. It's piping hot," the lady said.

"Oh no, we're fine. Thanks for the offer though," Sean said. Ivy gave a disapproving glare back at him, before taking her seat.

"Oh well, suit yourself. This dust you speak of. Do you have any of it on your person now?" Ivy asked.

"No, I used up the last of it that I had," Sheila said.

"Perfect. This will be loads of damn fun then, won't it? What color was the dust?" Ivy said.

"It was purple, in a beige drawstring bag," Sheila responded.

"Now we're getting somewhere. Tell me, was it lavender or a rich, dark purple?" she asked.

"It was definitely of a lavender hue. I remember that for sure," Sheila replied.

"Ok, that dust is used to ward off evil spirits that were not previously in the home yea. The tricky part is some houses already have a propensity for welcoming bad spirits, based on their history. Kind of like when you already have a sore throat and somebody coughs without covering their mouth in an enclosed space. Rude bastards. Ha! Two weeks later you get the flu. They were just the catalyst to the inevitable. Let me tell you for true, that dust wasn't going to help much if that was the case. How did you apply it?" Ivy asked, as she walked to the stove and poured a single serving of tea in her cup.

"That's the thing. I lined the front door first, then lined the edges of the inside of the house. Then, outside the door. Was that right?" Sheila asked, frightened at the possibility that she could have applied it wrong.

"Sounds like you did it right to me. You must remember that when it comes to voodoo, it's not a one-solution-fits-all process. The powder worked for your friend, but you must have a different type of situation. Otherwise, it would have worked for you just the same. Refresh my memory. Was your friend the one with the sister I told her to stay away from?" Ivy asked.

* * *

"Yes, that was her. I was there with her that night," Sheila said.

"Yes, you believed me, but she was more skeptical. You know they say it doesn't get to you if you fail to believe? How is that hell raiser sister of hers anyway? She was highly offended at my observations," Ivy chuckled.

"Um, her sister actually passed away a few months ago," Sheila responded solemnly. The air in the room was thick enough to cut with a knife and still have more to get through.

"Oh. I give my regards to the undertaker then," Ivy said dryly.

"Baby, let's go. We are wasting our time here. This woman is a fraud," Sean blurted out.

"Excuse me, mister. You know, it's not wise to call a woman like me a fraud. I'll chalk it up to your ignorance," Ivy cackled.

"Sean, let's just stay a few more minutes, then we'll go. I promise," Sheila said, grabbing his hand.

"Listen, I'll tell you this. Then, you can be on your merry way. I'm going to give you three cloves of fresh garlic. Put them in a sock, one at a time. Over the course of three days, put the next clove in the sock. Hang the sock over your bedroom door the first night, over the inside of your front door the second night and on the third night, put it in the freezer. Keep the garlic and the sock together and let it sit there for seven days. Then remove it. Don't just throw it away in your trash can. Drive it at least ten miles away from your home and then discard it there. Whatever you do, don't forget that last step. If you do, you will negate the entire ritual," Ivy said.

● ● ●

"Garlic? I don't think we have vampires," Sheila said. She was now beginning to feel like this was a mistake as well. Some Ivy's methods just seemed too farfetched, without any solid explanation.

"No, sweetie. My senses are telling me that vampires are the least of your concern. Trust me, you want to start this process right away. It's only going to get worse from here. So, it's up to you. Take my advice or take your chances walking through the forest with pork chop drawers on. It's your choice," Ivy said.

Chapter 22

Bill woke up the next morning and started sketching out the crib he was making for the new baby. He calculated all the measurements nearly in his head alone. Bill started making a sketch of the vision he had. He didn't want to chance running into that nosy detective again at Home Depot. So, he decided to go to Lowe's instead. The drive was a little further out, but he didn't have much to do that day.

He smiled nearly the whole way there, thinking about Cookie's first moments as a baby and her growing up over the years. Although he wasn't there during Chelsea's birth, he loved her just the same. He missed his daughter dearly. Bill and Lisa tried everything they could to help her. He often questioned if he was just too out of touch at some point in Chelsea's life. Maybe that was the reason her life ended the way it did.

Truth be told, he never really forgave himself for Chelsea's drug addiction. No parent wants their child to turn to drugs as a coping mechanism, let alone experience any kind of pain. Bill thought back to the first time he suspected something was going wrong with Chelsea. It was just a couple of months after her 19th birthday. Chelsea had come home from school for the summer. She only stayed at home for two weeks.

Chelsea and Cookie were always both self-sufficient. However, Chelsea would let Bill and Lisa baby her sometimes. Bill remembered how snappy and rude she was while she was at home. He chalked it up to teenage hormones and the new college experience. Had he paid more attention back then, maybe he could have helped her. Nevertheless, Bill still struggled to come to grips with the fact that Chelsea made her own decisions. Tragically, she paid for those decisions with her life.

Bill tried to shake the negative thoughts as he perused the isles of Lowe's to get a real-life picture of the items he would need to make the crib. He knew he would end up doing the same thing when he came to Dallas, but his OCD tendencies wouldn't let him rest until he mapped it all it out. Bill didn't have to wait much longer though. Cookie was due very soon and he would be in Dallas by the end of next week.

He walked through each isle with his pencil and notepad, sketching images and taking notes. One of the associates asked him if he needed anything, but he dismissed them more rudely than he meant to. He was just so in the zone and didn't really have time for anyone asking him questions to throw off his focus. Finally, Bill wrapped up his research at the store and decided to head back home.

There was traffic building up right before the exit he needed to take before getting home. Just as the traffic slowed to nearly a hault, his phone rang. It was Cathy calling him. "Goodness, what did this woman want now?" he thought. Bill exhaled deeply before he answered his phone.

"Hello? Cathy?" Bill answered, sounding pleasant, but inserting a bit of sternness to his tone.

"Oh, hi Bill. I hope I didn't disturb you. I know this may sound a little strange but I'm making a pot roast this evening. I'm also whipping up some mashed potatoes and some fresh green beans. I can't eat all this alone. I'm not sure if you've ever tried it, but I make a mean apple pie too. Everything should be ready

* * *

around 7:00 pm if you want to come by and grab a plate. I mean, you're more than welcome to stay and um, eat with me too if you'd like," she said.

"Thank you, Cathy," Bill said, pausing for a moment to collect his thoughts before he continued. "As delicious as that sounds, I'm expecting my grandchild any day now. I'll be hard at work on some ideas for a crib I'm building. You know these new aged parents. I don't even know if it's a boy or a girl yet. But I actually have some leftovers from what I cooked last night".

Bill was lying through his teeth. He didn't cook anything last night and he was pondering what he would prepare for dinner later that evening. He just didn't feel right having dinner with another woman in that setting, especially since he murdered her husband. His conscious wouldn't let him go through with it for more reasons than one.

"Well, isn't that precious? I know you are just going to spoil that baby beyond belief. I totally understand. Just thought I'd extend the offer. Sounds like you might be out on the road. If you want to just come by and pick up a plate, later I can have one ready for you," she said.

Bill really didn't want the food, but Cathy was being so persistent. He didn't want to completely let her down. "Ok, sure I'll do that. I can be there around 7:15 pm to pick up the plate. How does that sound?" he said.

"Great! That is perfect timing. Everything will still be piping hot by then. Ok, well I guess I will see you soon then sir," Cathy replied. Bill could sense that she was smiling on the other end.

* * *

"Ok, I will see you in a little bit. Thanks Cathy," Bill responded.

"Of course. You're very welcome Bill. Anytime. See you soon," Cathy said before she hung up the phone.

Bill drove home first and caught up on some ESPN highlights before heading over to Cathy's house. The last time he drove in that direction was when he killed Caldwell. He never really had a guilty conscious about it until now. That bastard deserved to die. Bill wished he had suffered more and really known what it felt like to rape his daughter, let alone anyone else he likely harmed. However, Cathy was lonely. All she knew was she lost her husband. For that, Bill did feel a bit of remorse.

When he arrived at the house, he called Cathy to let her know he was pulling up. "Well, don't just stay in the car. Come on in. The door is open. I'm finishing up your plate now, so you have perfect timing," Cathy said.

"Nice, ok. Well, sure. I'll go ahead and come in," Bill replied. He walked up to the door and turned the metal door knob handle to walk in. Everything was nearly just as Bill remembered. He half expected Caldwell to come out of the back room and announce his presence. The house felt eerie without him being there.

"I know you're a busy man, but I'm so glad you stopped by to get a plate. Do you think you may have some time to sit down and really enjoy your meal after all?" she inquired.

"No, I really do have to get going. Thanks again for the invite though. It smells delicious. I know it's going to be great," Bill responded. He was visibly starting to get annoyed with Cathy's persistence. He already told her he couldn't stay. She acted as if she never even heard him.

"I understand. If you insist. Here's a to go cup with some punch that I made to go with the meal. There's a secret ingredient in there. I'm telling you, you're going to love it," she said, securing the lid before handing him the cup.

"I can't wait to dig into this. Everything looks and smells so delicious. I really appreciate this Cathy," Bill said.

"That really makes an old lady like me feel good. You know, ever since I lost Caldwell, I still haven't gotten used to cooking for one person. There's still quite a bit left, even after your plate. I pack up some plates and take them to the church for the homeless. It would be a sin to try to hoard all of this myself. I like to think I'm bringing a smile to someone that needs it, or at least satisfying their hunger for a bit," Cathy replied, with a cracked voice. Bill could tell she was trying to hold herself together as best she could.

"Your crown in heaven will hold many jewels. You have a great heart Cathy. Thanks again. I really appreciate it," Bill said, slowly pacing towards the front door with his plate and drink in hand.

"Bill, I'm so lonely here. I'm not built for this. Things weren't always perfect between Bill and I. But this emptiness in this house is more than I can bear at times," she sobbed.

"I know it's difficult. I can't stand the way my house feels without Lisa either. But she's there in spirit and that gets me through it. I remember the good times. Caldwell is still here too. He's right here with you. I know he would never leave you alone," Bill

● ● ●

190

replied, giving Cathy a tight hug, with his right leg planted towards the door.

"I needed this, Bill. You are truly a Godsend. You go get started on that grandbaby's crib. I've kept you long enough," Cathy smiled, wiping the tears from her eyes, as she reluctantly pulled herself away from Bill's embrace.

"I'll go ahead and get going, but you will be ok. You're too good of a woman not to be. I'll talk to you later Cathy," Bill said as he turned the knob on the front door. He really did feel sorry for Cathy, but his heart would forever be with Lisa. He didn't want to take a chance on hurting her again, even in death.

"Thank you. You're a good man too Bill. Let me know what you think about the food. Be safe and have a good night," Cathy said.

"Sure, I will definitely do that. Thanks again," he replied.

Bill drove home in silence without the radio on. He needed to process everything that just happened. He still didn't feel any remorse for killing Caldwell. However, he did feel sorry for Cathy. She was now all alone and without a husband. Bill knew the feeling all too well when he lost Lisa. Maybe that was his payback; karma taking Lisa first and him still being around to suffer through it.

When Bill got home, he sat in his parked SUV before he got out. The robust fragrance from the food had now filled his entire vehicle. He looked down at the plate of food sitting the passenger seat and the drink in the cupholder. Bill took a peak inside the foil. He pulled off a piece of the roast and ate it. Cathy was an excellent cook. The food was seasoned just right. It tasted delicious.

Bill finally got out of the SUV, with his food and drink in tow. He turned on the kitchen light and sat everything down on the counter. He grabbed a plate out of the cupboard to divvy out a smaller portion of the food to eat. Cathy gave him too much to eat for just one serving. Bill started scooping generous portions of food on the plate to heat up in the microwave. Then, it hit him. What if this was all a ploy to get back at him for killing Caldwell? After all, Cathy did insinuate that she knew something about his death when he last spoke with her. Maybe this was her way of avenging her husband's murder.

Bill lived by the rule that you must be careful of whose food you eat. He especially wasn't fond of eating from the hands of a woman scorned. He didn't even like eating food that Lisa cooked for him when he knew she was upset with him. He scraped the food off the plate, into the trash can. Bill threw the rest of it away as well. He even poured the drink she prepared down the drain. If Cathy was up to no good, he refused to be taken down so easily.

He grabbed a frozen lasagna out of the deep freezer and warmed it in the oven. The lasagna wasn't exactly his idea of a home cooked meal. However, he didn't want to take the chance on any foul play by eating Cathy's food. Bill waited about 45 minutes, as he was taking the first bite of his lasagna, to text Cathy and tell her how wonderful the food was.

"Cathy, you really outdid yourself. The food was amazing. I'm very grateful. Thank you," Bill typed.

* * *

"Oh, yes! Thanks Bill. Anytime. Glad you enjoyed it," Cathy replied.

Bill took another bite of his food and took a swig of some Jack and Coke as he leaned back in his recliner. He turned on the TV and landed on a sitcom. He was content knowing that the food he was consuming wouldn't harm him. He smiled as the smell of the remnants of the homecooked food from Cathy and the cooked lasagna lingered in the living room.

❊ ❊ ❊

Chapter 23

Cookie sat at home on Sunday morning craving all kinds of foods, while Ken stepped out to go jogging. They worked out together during much of her pregnancy, but she wasn't feeling well enough for too much physical activity in the last couple of weeks. She was getting closer to the due date and she could feel every bit of the extra weight she gained. Her breath was shorter than ever before and it didn't take much to make her feel fatigued. The recent blood donor situation with Lance didn't make it better.

She was still upset with Ken for making such a big decision without consulting her first. Nonetheless, she had to admit that she would have been elated if a close friend (let alone godparent) stepped up like that for her child. So, she decided she would just suck it up for karma's sake. That didn't mean that she had to keep the situation to herself though.

There was plenty of food to eat in the kitchen, but she had a tough time deciding what she wanted. There was gelato in the freezer or she could make a peanut butter and jelly sandwich, with bananas and drizzle some honey on it. There was some left-over chicken alfredo from The Olive Garden in the refrigerator. Who was she kidding? She needed to find the simplest way to satisfy her craving with minimal effort. She thought about texting Ken to bring her some food when he got back from his jog. The request would have been wasted because she wasn't even sure of what she wanted.

Cookie rolled over on her right side and looked inside of her closest before walking into the kitchen. It was a nice distraction to catch her breath before she started walking. All her larger, maternity clothes were pushed to the front of the closet. Her sexy, slinky dresses were all pushed to the back. She envisioned herself being able to fit in them again one day. The doctor told her she was five pounds under the expected weight gain for a pregnant woman her age. Nevertheless, she just still felt like she was carrying so much weight around. After all, it was the largest she had ever been in her life.

Although she was going to be a big girl (in the figurative sense) and not continue to nag Ken about his actions, she had to vent to someone. Sheila had her own problems, trying to get those evil spirits out of her house. Renita would just tell her how she was right all along. Men were no good in her book; unless it was for sex. She even questioned the validity of that for some men. There was one person who would understand. This person would listen, without any judgment. Mike.

Cookie scrolled through her phone and realized Mike hadn't texted her back since she last reached out to him. That was odd, considering he was the one that initiated the conversation. Maybe he just wanted to say congratulations on her being pregnant and that was it. Maybe everything was just too awkward for him now, especially after recently getting married.

Oh well, she decided to text him anyway. She had to make it quick. Ken would likely be back home soon. "Hey Mike. This is Cookie. How are you?" Cookie stared at her phone, waiting for a response. How pathetic could one person be? She placed her phone on the counter as she poured herself a big bowl of Fruity Pebbles, with almond milk. She hoped Ken didn't need any of the

* * *

milk to make a smoothie when he got back, because she just used the last of it.

She glanced back at her phone as she carried her bowl of cereal to bed. Finally, she saw that Mike was typing something back to her. His reply appeared to be long, based on his response time. Cookie was wrong. He kept it simple. "Hey Cookie. I'm doing well. Nice to hear from you," he said.

Umph. He didn't even have the decency to ask her how she was doing. This conversation was not playing out the way she wanted it to go. He started typing again. She ate another spoonful of cereal, missing her mouth and spilling some of the milk on her plush pink robe.

"How is everything going with your pregnancy? You're going to be an excellent mother, Cookie. I know Ken will be a great dad too," he said. That was more like it.

"Thank you. That really means a lot. Only about three weeks left. I'm excited, cranky, emotional, ready to get it over with. You know, all of the normal pregnancy feelings, lol," Cookie responded. She felt a wave of peace and familiarity come over her. Mike always reminded her of what stability felt like. No matter what went on her life, he was always there to support her or lend a listening ear. Although he crossed the line years ago, it was really a one-sided friendship. Cookie never understood what he gained by remaining friends with her.

"Ah, you're being too hard on yourself. I'm sure you're handling it all like a champ and looking great while doing it," he said.

"I'm trying my best," she replied with a wide mouthed smiley face emoticon. "So, how's married life? How does it feel to be an ole tied down man now?" she continued.

"It's been a rollercoaster ride to say the least," he said.

"What? It's too early in the marriage for that kind of tone. You should be humping like rabbits and exploring new hobbies together. What's going on?" Cookie asked. Great. Instead of getting what she needed to off her chest, he was having problems too. Perhaps this was just karma paying her a visit for all the times she selfishly used him as her sounding board.

"Eh, it's a long story. I'd have to call you and tell you about it. Maybe we can meet up soon to discuss it," he responded.

"Um, I don't really have a sometime soon, lol. This baby is ready to pop. Come on, go ahead and tell me," she pleaded. Cookie saw Mike quickly typing his reply.

"Can you talk now?" Mike said.

"Um, yeah. I mean I think so. Ken just went out for a jog," Cookie said.

"Well, if you're not allowed to talk right now, we can just wait like I said," Mike replied curtly.

"Ugh, man just call me," Cookie typed back.

There was complete silence for a couple of minutes. Mike didn't text back. Then, suddenly he called her. "Hey. Hello?" Cookie answered nervously.

* * *

197

"Well, I must say I didn't exactly expect to hear from you, especially not this soon," he said.

"I texted you back the other day, but I didn't hear anything from you. Did you get it?" she said.

"Yeah I saw it. Just have a lot going on right now. Sorry about that," Mike retorted.

So, he did see it and just didn't respond to her. Cookie didn't know whether to feel more insulted or proud of him. It was one of those rare times that he failed to play by her rules. She liked it. She respected it. She was slightly embarrassed that it even turned her on.

"Oh, I got it. Well, go ahead. Spill it. What do you have to tell me?" Cookie replied. She tried to make it sound like she was totally unbothered that he failed to respond to her.

"Ok, I'll get straight to the point. I won't be married too much longer. We're separated," Mike said. There was a chilling silence on both ends of the phone.

"Um, what? Mike, I'm so sorry. What happened?" she said.

"It's such a long story, but I basically found out she was cheating on me," Mike said.

"Oh, hell no! That is so disrespectful. You know what? You're a great guy and it's her loss. She truly doesn't deserve you," Cookie replied.

"It's alright. It's life. I'm just so sick of this shit. This life is bullshit," Mike exclaimed.

● ● ●

"Whoa, wait a minute. Now you're talking crazy, Mike. Please don't say that. No relationship is worth jeopardizing your life," she said, with a harsh tone of concern.

"Don't worry. I'm not talking about ending my life. Don't dial the suicide hotline. It's not that serious. I mean that I'm just sick of being the nice guy. I guess it's true what they about nice guys finishing last," Mike replied.

"Come on now, Mike. That's not true. She's just not the one. That bitch. I could really slap her around, since you can't hit her," Cookie chuckled.

"You know what, Cookie? I'm such a nice guy that I can see through the bullshit you're spewing right now," he said.

"What? Excuse me? Mike, that was low. What are you talking about?" Cookie responded, genuinely confused.

"You know what I'm talking about. Cookie, you never just check on me. We've been friends for how long now? I know the MO. There's something you want to tell me. So, you spill it. I'm all ears, as always," he replied in an agitated tone.

"Mike, I really was concerned about how you were doing, especially when I didn't get a text back from you the other day. Besides the stuff that I have going on really pales in comparison. I shouldn't even mention it," Cookie uttered softly.

"Goodness, Cookie. Cut the bullshit. Now what do you have to tell me?" Mike said, breathing hard into the phone.

"Alright, ok. You don't have to be so hostile about it. It's Ken. I just don't know where to start. It's a weird situation. He's got this godson. Sweetest little boy. He really is adorable. Very energetic and the whole nine. He got sick. He needs a blood transfusion now. It's urgent for his health, you know. Well, Ken just so happens to have the blood type he needs. So, he told his best friend that he agreed to give blood for him," Mike said.

"Ok, I don't hear anything wrong yet. Sounds like he's just being a stand-up guy like he always is," he said, shaking his head, listening to Cookie rant.

"Well, I'm not finished yet. He made the decision without consulting me first. Don't you think that's ludicrous?" she exclaimed.

"I get it that it makes you upset. It would probably sting a little for me too. I'll give you that. Cookie he's doing the right thing. Are you upset that he's doing it period, or just that you didn't know first?" he said. Truth be told, he could totally see her point. He couldn't give in though. That would just fire her up even more. Plus, he was still angry with her and didn't feel like consoling her.

"I just hate it when you're right. I know I shouldn't feel so strongly about this. I guess it just hurt my feelings. That's a big decision to make without telling your spouse. You're always my voice of reason. I can see I was over reacting now," Cookie replied calmly.

"No worries. Your bill is in the mail," he laughed.

"Oh, you've got jokes. Too funny. Well, I would love for you to meet the baby. It should be here soon. Really, any day now," Cookie beamed.

"Wait a minute. Did you just say "it"? Either you and Ken are expecting Pennywise Jr or you must be one of those new age

parents that wants to find out the sex of the baby the day of,"
Mike joked.

"Um, it would be the latter sir. Pennywise Jr. Goodness. Get out
of here. You are still crazy, I see. We both decided we would just
wait to find out what the sex would be. You're not the only one
that disagrees with it. Most people think we are crazy. But back
to you. Don't let that woman get you down. You're going to make
it through this smelling like roses. You watch and see," she said.

"I'm glad you have so much faith in me. I really appreciate that
Cookie. Thanks for checking up on me, even if it was for your own
selfish motives," Mike snickered.

"Oooh, you are really driving the digs in today. I'll let you make it
this time," Cookie laughed back.

"Seriously, it's nice to hear from you. After I made a fool of
myself, I didn't think you wanted to have anything else to do with
me. I'm sure the hubby will be home soon though. I'll talk to you
later," Mike replied.

"Ok, well it was really good speaking to you too Mike. Oh, and I
never said you made a fool of yourself. Love you boy. Take care,"
Cookie said.

"Yeah, you too. Take care, Cookie," Mike replied, dumbfounded
at Cookie's response. Did she love him as more than a friend?
Maybe he had a better shot at having her back then than he
realized. He quickly snapped out of it and came back to reality.
Mike was never going to have Cookie as his own.

• • •

Chapter 24

The next few days flew by. Cookie kept telling Ken that she felt like the baby was going to come early. However, he had a hunch that the baby would arrive past the due date. Things were tense that morning when he woke up. The time had come for him to give blood for Lance. He cooked dinner for Cookie the night before, but she sensed it was just his way of trying to get back in her good graces. It did work somewhat, but she was still upset.

"Alright babe, I'm about to head over to the hospital now to give the blood. I'll be back in a little bit," Ken said.

"Ok, honey. Thanks again for the dinner last night. It was really delicious," Cookie replied.

"Thanks. I'm glad you enjoyed it. I aim to please. I'll call you when I get there," Ken responded.

"Sounds good. I'll be here waiting. Not like I can run off and go anywhere," she laughed sarcastically, looking down at her very pregnant belly. "Hey. I never asked, but what's the recovery time for you giving blood?"

"Cookie, come on now. You know Lance needs this. I can't turn my back on that little boy now," he replied defensively.

"Calm down. I'm not saying that at all. I know Lance needs it. I get that and I'm not trying to stop you from helping him at all. Ken, we do have a child of our own coming into this world too. We've got two weeks, maybe less. That's it. I can't do this by myself. I just want to make sure you'll be feeling back to your regular self by then," Cookie retorted.

* * *

"Everything will be just fine, baby. I'm healthy, so the recovery time will be even less for me, I'm sure. It takes up to six weeks for all the blood to repair itself in the body. That doesn't mean I'm going to pass out or be sick or anything like that Cookie. I'm going to be ok. I promise," he said, walking over to sit next to her on the bed.

"I can't lose you, Ken. I believe you and I hope that everything will be ok. You and my dad are all I have left. I need you here, especially with this little bundle of joy on the way," Cookie said, smiling at Ken through her tears.

"You're not losing me. This is forever. I meant that when I said it at the alter on our wedding day. If I have to take several five-hour energy shots and they have to roll me into the hospital room, I'm going to be there for our baby. There is no way I would neglect you or the baby," Ken reassured her.

"I'm sorry. I know you are only doing the right thing. I've kept you long enough. You better get going. The quicker you get there, the quicker you'll get back to me. Tell Lance I love him and he's going to be ok," Cookie said.

"I will do that baby. I love you and I'll see you soon," Ken said.

"I love you more. You're going to make a great father. I'm sure of it," Cookie said, wiping the last traces of tears from her cheeks.

"Only with you by my side as the best mother ever. See you soon babe," Ken replied.

Ken locked the door and took a big swig of water from a bottle he grabbed from the kitchen. Truth be told, Ken was nervous about giving blood to Lance. Cookie had a valid point. He had never given blood before and was unsure of what to expect. Ken felt the sweat of his palms on the steering wheel as he drove to the hospital. He turned the radio on to help distract him from his racing thoughts. Before he knew it, he was already pulling into to the parking garage at the hospital. His phone sounded a text message alert as he was finding his parking spot.

Ken waited a couple of minutes until he was parked. He figured it was just Cookie worried about him. She probably was just checking to see if he made it there safely. To Ken's surprise, the text was from Alicia. He quickly picked up the phone to read the text. As eager as he was to read the message, he did the right thing and let Cookie know he made it there first.

"Ken, please call me as soon as you get this. I need to talk to you before you get here. Before Charles sees you. It's urgent," Alicia texted. Dammit. This was the last thing he needed; more drama. Ken tried to remain optimistic as he dialed Alicia's phone number.

"Ken, is that you?" Alicia asked nervously.

"Hey, yeah it's me. Is Lance ok? I called as soon as I got your text," Ken responded.

"Yeah, Lance is fine. It's Charles. He's really not good right now," Alicia responded, her voice lowering its tone. She sounded like she was in a hollow room and purposely trying to whisper.

"Well, what happened?" Ken asked.

"He knows Ken. He just found out!" Alicia said. Ken would have given anything at that moment not to hear those words.

"Huh? Wha....? How could you tell him? What in the hell were you thinking? Do you know what this is going to do to me?" he yelled.

"You? Is that all you can think about right now? I have to deal with this too! Look, he found out from one of the nurses. She remembered Lance and I. She kept giving me this strange look. She said she knew me and she told Charles I was a bad woman. Said I was ungrateful to have a husband as great as him. I have no idea what she told him," Alicia said.

"Dammit. How did Charles find out then?" Ken said, looking around in the parking garage, as he continued interrogating Alicia.

"He knew, Ken. He just knew. When he came back and I saw that expression of utter disgust on his face, that gave it away. I had to come clean and tell him. I'm sorry. I promise, I'm not trying to ruin your and Cookie's life. We will get through this. I know we will," Alicia assured him.

"Whatever. Shit. I'm on my way in. I'll just have to deal with Charles when I see him," he said. Ken hung up the phone without giving Alicia a chance to respond. He quickly walked into the hospital to get the process started to offer his blood. Ken asked which holding room Lance was in and made his way to him. Ken hated that he would have to see Charles like this. However, he couldn't back down now. No matter what happened, he had to fulfill his promise.

Ken barely made his way out of the elevator, when he saw Charles storming towards him. Ken had never seen a fire like that in his best friend's eyes before. "You've got some damn nerve for lying to me after all these years. I swear if it weren't for you giving Lance this blood, I would bash your head into the ground right now!" Charles screamed.

"Charles, I know we can't undo the past. I never wanted you to find out like this. I'm so sorry," Ken responded, in a daze.

"Who the hell do you think you are? Undo the past? You're going to go in there and give this blood to my son. Yes, I said my son because you haven't done shit for him. After this, I don't ever want to see your face again," Charles said curtly.

"I understand. Um, where should I go to see Lance or to get everything started?" Ken asked.

"Follow me," Charles said, turning around without looking back at Ken.

They walked down the hallway and turned right. Ken could see Alicia sitting outside a room at the end of the hallway. Her head was in her hands and she kept wiping her eyes. She looked up to see Ken and Charles coming towards her direction.

The doctor stepped out of the room where Lance was. Ken caught a glimpse of his face and saw his nervousness. He wanted to console him but figured now wasn't a good time. "Ah, so you must be Ken; the man of the hour. Glad you made it on time. I'm Dr. Birchen," he said, extended his hand to shake Ken's.

"Yes, that's me. Here to help Lance. He's quite a trooper. I'm just glad to be able to get him back to normal. He's such an active young man," Ken replied.

* * *

206

"Well, yes even after knowing him for such a brief time, I can see he is an amazing ball of energy. I know Charles and Alicia here have go to be some very grateful parents," Dr. Birchen smiled.

"Oh yes, we are just thrilled. Ecstatic to receive such a warm act of kindness from such a great and trusted friend. Aren't we happy honey?" Charles said stiffly, wrapping his arm around Alicia's shoulder in a forceful manner.

Alicia could barely speak. She shook her head yes in agreement. No one said a word for a few seconds. That quick window of time felt like an eternity. Dr. Birchen sensed the tension and broke the ice by bringing everyone in to see Lance before Ken got prepped to give blood.

Chapter 25

"Girl, I'm so glad this is the last day of this damn garlic ritual," Sheila said, laughing with Cookie.

"I know you are. I bet your house smells like garlic everywhere too," Cookie joked.

"Hey, I would have done this and more to make sure these spirits get the hell out of here. I guess that old bat knows what she's talking about," Sheila responded.

"Whatever works to get rid of that stuff. That was really beginning to scare me. You know I'm not easily spooked," Cookie said.

"I know. Tell me about it. I was so close to telling Sean that we would just have to sell this house and find somewhere else to live," Sheila agreed.

"Hey, Sheila. There's something I need to tell you about that whole thing. You know when you told me you saw my sister's face? Well, I saw it too the other day. I almost hit this lady walking across the parking lot at work. Her face looked just like Chelsea's. It was so uncanny, and it made me nervous the rest of the day. I turned around and looked at the lady again. Clearly it wasn't her. At that moment, I felt like I was looking right at her," Cookie confessed.

"I've seen her face too. Maybe there's something she needs to tell us. I don't know," Sheila answered.

"What do you mean? What could she possibly have to say?" Cookie replied in a concerned voice.

* * *

"Oh, I don't know Cookie. You know how in those movies people always say the dead come back to say their last words? I have no idea what she would want to say. I know you've got to miss your baby sister," Sheila responded.

"Girl, do you know how much that would spook me out if Chelsea decided to come back for some last words? I love her and I miss her dearly. Something reminds me of Chelsea every single day. Even the scent of some foods make me think of her. She's all around me. I can't escape it. Truth be told, the pregnancy has been a nice distraction. All of my thoughts were beginning to consume me," Cookie said.

"Well, you are one of the strongest women I know. You wouldn't let that happen. Plus, I wouldn't let you. You're about as close to me as sisters will ever get. Cookie, you are like blood to me and I'm not letting you walk this road alone," Sheila said softly. She felt a chill dance down her spine as she walked out of her bedroom where the sock with garlic dangled from the door frame.

"Don't make me cry. I get heartburn every time I start crying now. Goodness, I'll be glad when this part is over with. I can't remember the last time in my life that I cried this much on a consistent basis," Cookie laughed.

"Hey, appreciate it while you can. After the baby, you'll have to deal with your breasts leaking all over the place," Sheila laughed.

"You always know how to find the silver lining. Oh, Ken just texted me. He should be back home soon," Cookie smiled.

* * *

"That's right. You did say he was supposed to give Lance blood today. That is just so noble of him. I know it's his godson, but not a lot of people would do that. Plus, right before you have the baby. Ken has a really good heart," Sheila added.

"Yeah, he does. Sheila, can I ask you something?" Cookie inquired.

"Shoot. Of course. What's that?" Sheila responded curtly.

"It's actually about Ken. He made the decision to donate blood to Lance without telling me first. I know it may seem petty, but I was so upset with him about that. I'm over it now, but I just want to know if I even had a right to be mad about it," Cookie replied softly.

"Wait. So, did he tell you the same day he decided to do it?" Sheila asked calmly.

"Yes, he told me. It was the same day that they threw the baby shower for me at work. Was I wrong for feeling like he should have told me first?" Cookie asked.

"You know I hate to tell you when you're wrong. I really do. Although a little piece of me inside really loves it. Cookie, I'm afraid this is one of those times. Girl, he told you right after it happened. What is the big deal? It's not like he bought a car and just showed up with it in the driveway. That's something to be mad about. This is just those hormones talking. As soon as you give birth, you'll see. All the pettiness and sensitivity will be released from you. I declare it now," Sheila snickered.

● ● ●

"Ugh, you know I hate it when you are right. You're the second person who told me this," Cookie uttered. She immediately regretted her words as soon as they escaped her lips.

"Just take it easy. You have a good man. You and Ken are expecting a healthy baby and building a family. A lot of people would kill to be in your shoes. Don't make a mountain out of a molehill," Sheila cautioned.

"Well, aren't you the wise one?" Cookie joked.

"I do what I can," Sheila laughed back.

"Alright then, girl. Ken should be here soon. I'll see how he feels when he gets in. Hopefully he's not too weak from giving the blood. Thanks again for listening and talking some sense in to me. I appreciate it more than you know," Cookie said.

"You know I always have your back. You're my sister. Get ready for Ken. I think we finally have this house voodoo proof now. Thank goodness. I'll talk to you later," Sheila replied.

"Yes, I am so glad all of those bad spirits are getting out of your house now. Who knows? You and Sean may be next to be visited by the stork," Cookie smiled.

"Ooh, don't conjure that up yet. Sean is readier than I am. I'm just not ready to give up my selfish ways yet. I'm getting there, slowly but surely though. You know you will be the first to know if it does happen though. Oh, maybe we can grab lunch in the next few days. I know you've been so busy, but you gotta slow down now that the baby is on the way," Sheila urged.

"That should work out perfectly. My dad will be here Tuesday, so I should be free before then. I know, believe me I am trying to slow down and de-stress as much as I can. I'm a work in progress. That's for sure. I'm sure we'll talk before then," Cookie replied.

"Most definitely. Take care and tell Ken I said hi," Sheila said.

"I will and you tell Sean I said hello too. Bye," Cookie responded. She let out a deep, hearty sigh as she hung up the phone. That was the second confirmation she received that maybe she was being too hard on Ken. After all, he never gave her a reason to distrust him. Even when he slept with Melissa, she somehow believed his story right off. Maybe she was blinded by love or maybe he was really the perfect man for her. She chose to believe in the latter.

Cookie decided to turn on the TV, while she waited for Ken to get home. She figured he would be there soon, based on the time of his text message. She clicked through the channels and ended up landing on the music video for TLC's "Creep". She laughed to herself and remembered her and Chelsea doing the routine together. There was no way she could do that routine now even if she tried. Instead, she just flailed her arms to the beat as she sat on the couch.

She really missed her sister. Tears began to stream down her face as she stared at the music video playing on the TV screen. She told herself to stop being so sensitive and snap out. Cookie quickly turned the channel and landed on an episode of *This Is Us*. Nope. That wasn't something she needed to see right then either. She eventually stopped on a Netflix documentary about nature.

Ken pulled into the garage a few minutes later. Cookie heard him let the garage back down, but it took him a while to come in the house. She hoped everything was ok, but then told herself to stay calm and not panic. She figured he may have been talking to Charles on the way home. Cookie knew she had been a handful these last few weeks. Hell, she couldn't blame him if he was trying to clear his mind before coming in the house. She was tired of even being around herself at times.

Finally, the lock turned and she heard him walk in from the garage into the kitchen. "There's my baby!" Cookie exclaimed. Once again, she had to coach herself inside her mind. "Goodness, let the man breathe before he comes in," she told herself.

"Hey baby. How's my Queen doing?" Ken said nervously.

"Ooh, well I don't really feel like anybody's royalty right now. However, I think I could get used to the sound of that title," she smiled. Cookie rolled to her side and pushed herself off the couch to greet her husband. She took one look in his eyes and immediately knew something was wrong. The whites of his eyes were spotted with red in the corners. She figured it was related to his blood donation but had a hunch it was something more.

Ken just smiled at her and hugged her tightly. She could feel his hot tears dripping on her shoulder. Cookie pulled him back so she could see his face again. She hoped that nothing went wrong with the procedure. Cookie knew she would feel like a complete jerk if that were the case. "Um, come on, let's sit down on the couch," she said.

"Alright," Ken uttered. He buried his eyes in the palms of his hands, taking a deep breath before looking Cookie directly in her

* * *

eyes. She could feel his breathing was staggered. She grabbed his right hand; it was sweaty and clammy.

"Ken, talk to me. I've never seen you like this. You're really scaring me. What's wrong?" Cookie said.

"Ok, I'll tell you. I guess I can't delay this any longer. Cookie, there's something you need to know about Lance," he said.

Cookie looked back at him with a perplexed expression. "Oh no, what happened? Did everything go ok? You're probably really dehydrated. Let me get you a glass of water. Sorry I didn't think of that when you first came in," Cookie said. Her hands were trembling so hard, she could barely open the cupboard.

"Baby, do you mind coming back over please? Lance is ok. But there's something else I need to tell you about him," Ken sighed.

"Ok, what's that?" Cookie asked, slowly walking back towards the couch.

"He's my son," Ken replied. Cookie stared at Ken so intently that her eyes pierced through him like lasers. She must have misheard him. There was no way her husband just told her that he was the biological father of a boy that was supposed to be his godson.

"I'm sorry. I must have heard you incorrectly. Could you repeat that again?" Cookie said calmly. She was trying to keep her composure, but her emotions were a steeping tea pot ready to blow.

"Lance is my son, Cookie. He's not my godson. I am his father, not Charles," he cried.

• • •

"No, no, no! There's no time for tears now. You managed to keep this lie a secret from me all this time, so you don't get the luxury of breaking down in tears now! What made you tell me now? Did Charles find out? Did you just want to clear your conscious before we had our baby? I'll be damned. Everybody was wrong. I should have trusted my instincts about you all along," she replied sternly. Ken's eyes were spilling over with water at this point. Meanwhile, there wasn't a single tear that dropped from Cookie's eyes.

"It all came out at the hospital. Apparently, there was a nurse there that remembered Alicia. She made a comment about Lance's birth and Charles put two and two together. I hadn't gotten to the hospital at that point. For the record, I didn't cheat on you with her. It only happened one time. I messed up bad. I never meant to sleep with my best friend's wife," he sobbed.

"Oh, but you meant to hurt your wife by not telling her and keeping it a secret until you were caught? I swear I couldn't catch a break in life if I tried. I thought I finally found the right man and come to find out that he already has a family. How can you sit back and neglect your son? Your son! Huh? Answer me! Then, you have me smiling in Alicia's face. I thought that bitch was my friend. I hate you," she said.

"Come on baby. Please, you don't mean that. I'm so sorry. I know you probably do hate me. I didn't mean to lie to you. I really didn't. I just thought that you were so perfect and I didn't want to hurt my chances with you. That's it. No more secrets," Ken said.

"Oh, well woop-de-fucking-doo. I should count my lucky stars that this is the only lie I have to deal with. After all, everyone else

● ● ●

tells me that all men do is lie. I guess I should just be content and happy with only one," Cookie replied.

"Come on, Cookie. To be fair, I didn't know about Brandon either when I first met you, or the miscarriage," he said.

"You've got some damn nerve, trying to compare that to this. Don't try to flip this around. I had to get rid of Brandon because he was abusive. My life was at stake and it was either him or me. I mean, what was I supposed to do? The miscarriage isn't even in the same fucking ocean, let alone the same boat!"

Cookie caught an explosive burst of energy and stormed out of the living room. Ken waited a couple of seconds before getting up to follow her. He knew she was devastated and rightfully so. He just didn't know how to fix it. "Baby, where are you going?" Ken asked softly.

"You don't get to ask the questions anymore. I don't have to answer to you. As a matter of fact, I don't want you anywhere near me and my baby. Just get out of our lives. Get out!" she exclaimed. Cookie started rummaging through the bedroom closet. She was tossing things around like a mad woman. Cookie turned around to see Ken standing at the opening of the closet, staring at her. His eyes were wells of emotion and his face was visibly trembling. It was the last thing she remembered before she blacked out.

• • •

Chapter 26

Bill hammered the last few nails of the crib down, before he sanded down some of the areas he missed. He stood back and admired his work. "Sweetheart, if you feel up to it, come take a look at this crib. This looks pretty awesome, if I do say so myself," Bill called out to his daughter.

"Ok, dad. I'll be right there," Cookie replied. She had been in a daze for the last few days. She tried to keep up a façade at home, without Ken being there. However, she felt like her soul was slowly eroding. Her due date was four days away, so she guessed Ken won the bet of when the baby would come. The house felt so awkward with just her and her dad there. But she was grateful that she wasn't in the house alone. She had been thinking more about the baby's sex lately. She and Ken agreed on the name Breanna if it was a girl and Brenton if it was a boy.

Cookie waddled as quickly as she could into the garage. Her dad immediately gave her a mask to put over her face. He didn't want her breathing in any of the saw dust from his work on the crib. Cookie felt special still being daddy's little girl, even though she was a grown woman expecting her own child. Cookie slipped the mask on and stepped into the garage. "Oh, my God," she gasped. "Dad, this is even more beautiful than I could have imagined. I love it. I'm sure Ken will love it too." The thought of Ken made her tears flow even stronger.

"So, does that mean you approve?" Bill asked with a wide smile, rubbing the side of the crib with his bare hands.

"Yes, I absolutely love it. We couldn't have bought a better crib," she cried. Cookie walked over to give her dad a hug, as she continued to cry. Her tears damped his shirt as she laid her head on his chest.

"Baby, let's go inside the house. You should probably be sitting down. I'll get you a glass of water," he said.

"Okay, that sounds good," she replied. Cookie became childlike again and very soft-spoken. She could sense that her father knew something was wrong.

"Candy, come on now. Be straight with me. What really happened to Ken? Why is he in the hospital? You've barely said a word about him. That's no way for a pregnant woman to act towards her husband days before she's due to give birth," he said sternly, staring at her directly in her eyes.

"Daddy. It's so complicated. I don't think you would understand. I don't want you to hate Ken," she sobbed.

"Try me. Did he hit you or cheat on you?" Cookie asked.

"No. It's not anything like that," she said. She figured she wouldn't dare go into the whole Melissa situation. Cookie didn't even have the energy to explain that in detail.

"Ok, well we're already starting off good. I can put my gun away now. You know, marriage is difficult. Your mother made me the happiest man alive, but we had our fair share of trials. Some were caused by me, some caused by her and some things were due to no one's fault. Disagreements and difficulties in marriage are inevitable. Show me a person that has a marriage that's always all peaches and cream, and I'll show you a liar," he said.

* * *

"Ken already has another child. I found out a few days before you got here. I didn't react too well and….," she said, before she got cut off.

"Wait a damn minute! What kind of shit is this? Where is he? I'm taking your car and I'm going to find him right now," Bill interjected. Cookie knew he was fuming, because he barely ever used profanity in her presence. She needed to diffuse his anger before he acted upon it.

"Whoa, I don't think we'll need to do that. I am ashamed to admit that I shot him. It was just a flesh wound. He's ok. I told him to get out. I blacked out after it happened. I don't remember much after that," Cookie confessed.

"Oh, my goodness. Well, I taught you well. Sounds like you gave him a good punishment. As much as I hate to accept it now, he is going to be the father of your child that's coming in a few days. Believe me, I didn't always do the best things in regards to your mother when she was here. I tried to shield you and your sister from that, but things were difficult for a time," he said.

"Are you saying I should just forgive him and move on?" Cookie asked.

"I'm not saying that at all. At the end of the day, you have to do what helps you sleep at night. When did all of this happen? If it's been since you and he were together, then you may want to think long and hard about staying," Bill responded.

"It was way before we were together. It's his godson. I just feel like such a fool. Lance's mother and Ken's best friend, Charles, who is her husband, were just at our house too. I can only

* * *

imagine how Charles is feeling right now. He keeps texting and calling me, begging for another chance. I'm just not ready yet. I feel so humiliated. Why couldn't he just be honest with me and tell me from the beginning?" Cookie asked.

"Ok, well that's at least good news that it happened before you met. He should have told you. That is true. Cookie, but, he wasn't the only one with skeletons in the closet. Yours just happened to fall out before they could be stuffed back in," he said.

"Ouch. Ok, I guess you have a good point there. I'll give him a call later," Cookie said. She suddenly felt a sharp kick inside of her womb. Her breath became short and she was starting feel light headed. The kicking was a throbbing feeling now and it intensified with every second. Goodness, it must be time.

"Candy, are you ok, baby?" Bill asked, quickly noticing the change of expression on his daughter's face.

"I um, I think it's time, daddy. Can you call Ken for me to meet us at the hospital?" she panted. Cookie could barely get the words out of her mouth. She leaned on the couch to stand up as her dad held on to her to walk her towards the car.

"Ok, take it easy. I got you. Lean all your weight on me. Anything you need out of here before we go?" he asked, walking with her and guiding her to the passenger seat of the car.

"Oh, thanks for asking. I probably would have forgotten. Just my purse and the purple bag in the bedroom. Everything I need is in there. Thank you, daddy. I love you," she said.

"I love you too, baby. Let's get your situated in the car first and then I'll go get your things. The grandbaby is on the way!" he smiled. For a moment, seeing her father's excitement made her totally forget about her ill feelings towards Ken.

Cookie grabbed her phone and started dialing Ken. She connected him to the car's Bluetooth system so she wouldn't have to hold the phone to hear ear. "Ken, hey it's me. The baby is um. Baby's on the way. My Dad and I are on the way to the hospital now," she said.

"Right now?! Ok, I'm on my way baby. I'll be right there. I can't wait. Love you," Ken said. Cookie could hear him quickly shuffling his keys in the background.

"Son, we'll see you there," Bill said. He remembered that feeling of being a new father just like it was yesterday. Now wasn't the time for him to be rude to Ken. He wasn't going to get away with lying to his daughter. However, Bill didn't want to rob him of that moment.

Bill was a smooth driver. Although he averaged about 85 miles per hour, he avoided any sudden turns or hard stops. Finally, they arrived at the hospital. They rushed Cookie in to the hospital and got her set up with a room to prepare to deliver the baby. She prayed that she would be able to have a natural birth. That's what she wanted. She smiled through her pain as she remembered Ken being so supportive.

The doctor asked if the father was coming. Bill interjected and confirmed that Ken was on his way. "Um, sweetie do you know about how far away Ken is from the hospital?"

* * *

"I don't know exactly where he's staying. Probably a hotel nearby. Not at Charles's house, for sure," she mumbled through her contractions.

"He needs to come on. Hopefully he'll be here soon," Bill replied impatiently.

"Oh, dad, can you take my phone and text Sheila? I promised her I would let her know when I was going into labor. It should still be inside of the bag," she requested.

"Sure, I'll take it. Let me go in the hallway. I'll be right back," Bill said.

He looked for Sheila's number to text her about Cookie going into labor. As soon as he sent the message, he looked through her logged calls to contact Ken. Now he was losing faith in Ken and felt silly for even taking up for him. "What kind of man isn't front and center at the hospital when his wife is about to deliver their baby?" he thought.

The phone rang three times before Ken answered. "Hello? Ken! Where are you? You need to make your way here quickly. She's here. The baby is coming," he said. No response. Bill pulled the phone back from his ear and looked at the screen. Ken didn't say a word. Bill became infuriated. He waited a couple of seconds longer before talking again. He heard a distant siren in the background. Maybe he was close by. "Hey, you just get here fast if you can hear this!"

Bill could feel his face turning red, but he tried to contain himself before walking back into the room. He didn't want to upset

• • •

223

Cookie any more than she probably already was. The doctor greeted him at the door as soon as he walked in.

"Hello sir, I'm Dr. Tinton. Your daughter is in great hands. Will you be here for a while? I understand her husband is on the way?" he said.

"Yeah I just called him. I don't know what he's doing but he should be here soon. I'm not leaving. I'll be here," Bill answered dryly.

"Ok, well that's good you'll still be here. You know, she may be here for a while, especially since she wants to have the birth naturally. Since she's a first-time mother, we expect a lengthy labor window here," Dr. Tinton said.

"Ha, you're pretty funny. I'll be here for however long it takes. I've been through this before. I'm old enough to have been in the delivery room when you were born. How old are you; 37...38?" Bill asked.

"I understand sir; it's just customary procedure that we let you know. I'm actually 43 years old," Dr. Tinton responded with a tinge of curtness. He then directed his attention back to Cookie and asked her how she was feeling.

"Candice, we are going to go ahead and get started with your delivery. We're going to try a natural birth, but I do have to warn you that we may have to explore other methods if that doesn't work," he said.

"It's going to be ok baby. Ken's on his way and you have me too. I'm right here. I'm not going anywhere," Bill said, rubbing Cookie's hand.

* * *

Meanwhile, Ken was trying to utter words back to Bill. He wasn't sure if he could even hear him. Miraculously, Ken's Bluetooth was still in his ear although his vehicle was flipped completely upside down. Somehow, it answered when Bill called him. He could barely make any audible noises. The impact of the flip was ringing heavily on the right side of his head. He felt like his head was a dented bowling bowl. Ken couldn't even see straight in front of him. Although he couldn't see everything around him, the person who clipped the tail end of his car appeared to be nowhere in sight. He still had to find a way to get to the hospital to be there for Cookie and the birth of their baby. He silently prayed that someone would quickly come to his rescue.

* * *

Chapter 27

Sheila handed Sean a homemade cocktail as soon as he walked in the door. He had just gotten home from a basketball tournament at the gym. By the look on his face, his team had won. "There she is. Look at my beautiful lady. Look at you. You must have sensed that there was cause for a special occasion," he said taking the drink from her and giving her a kiss.

"Yes, you could say that. You don't have much time to down that drink, though," Sheila replied.

"Oh really? I can chug it right now if that means I get to drink your waters next," he said, biting his bottom lip and staring deeply into her eyes.

"I hate to kill the mood. I will take you up on that later. Cookie's having the baby. I didn't want to just say, "Come on let's go," as soon as you got home. I figured I would soften the blow by making you a drink first. Oh, congratulations, baby. My man's got skills. I knew you would win," Sheila said.

"Ok, yeah let's get ready to go then," Sean said, sitting his gym bag down by the garage door and taking a big swig of the drink. "Damn, is this a Long Island Iced Tea? My favorite. I love you woman. Alright, I'm ready," he said.

"I take it that you approve of the drink. I'm glad you like it," she laughed as he gulped the last of the generous amount still left in the glass.

"Yes, I do. That hit the spot," he said. Ken grabbed a granola bar out of the pantry before he and Sheila made their way to the car.

* * *

"I'll drive us there. Good thing we only stay 15 minutes away from the hospital. I figure we can just go for moral support and then come back if it takes too long. I don't mind coming back by myself, if needed," she said.

Sheila and Sean hopped in the car. Sean turned on the radio and mentioned how excited and Ken must be to be a new father. She took it as another subtle hint that Sean was ready for them to start a family of their own.

"Yeah, I know he's got to be ecstatic. Funny thing though, her dad was the one that texted me. I thought it would have been Ken. Who knows? He could have been tied up or trying to calm Cookie down. I wonder if she's going to be one of those dramatic first-time moms. You know, screaming in agony and yelling at the doctor, "I am pushing, dammit!" Lord, please don't let that be me when it's my time," she said.

"You are something else. You know Cookie would curse you out if she heard you making fun of her like this," Sean laughed.

"Hey, I'm just saying. You know that's how a lot of new mothers are. Cookie's strong though. She is probably in there handling it like a champ," she responded.

"Yeah, you're right. I'm sure she is too," Sean said, looking out of the window. As soon as they pulled into the hospital, there was an ambulance parked right in front of the ER entrance. The paramedics were moving quickly to get the person on the stretcher inside out of the ambulance and into the hospital. Meanwhile, Sheila was looking for a parking spot.

* * *

"Goodness. Why are hospital parking garages always so full?" she mumbled to herself.

"Wait, baby. Hold on," Sean said, staring hard into his passenger mirror. He turned around in his seat to make sure what he was seeing was accurate.

"Everything ok, babe? Do you see a better spot somewhere?" Sheila asked, oblivious to what Sean was staring at. He remained silent and kept looking intently, without responding to Sheila. She abruptly stopped the car and followed his gaze.

"Sheila, tell me that's not Ken they are wheeling into the ER on that stretcher," Sean said.

"I really want to believe that's not him that I'm seeing too. That looks like him from here though. We must be too far away to really see. That can't be him, right? He would be inside the hospital with Cookie," Sheila replied. She wanted to believe that wasn't Ken, but it would explain why Bill was the one that texted her. They were too far away to tell for sure, but the man on the stretcher had a similar physique and skin color to Ken. Plus, Sheila recognized the gray boots the guy was wearing. Ken wore them often and she always thought they were so unique, because she never saw another man wear them.

"That can't be him baby. Why would he not be in the delivery room with Cookie and Bill? That would make no sense at all," Sean replied. He sounded more like he was trying to convince himself than ease Sheila's wondering mind. Sheila quickly found a parking spot and they walked briskly towards the ER opening. The paramedics still had the stretcher at the kiosk. Sean and

* * *

Sheila walked in as soon as they were about to wheel the person on the stretcher into a room.

They came in just a hair too late to be able to casually walk behind the stretcher. However, Sean caught a glimpse of the guy's right shoulder. It was exposed, due to a tear in his shirt and he noticed the same tattoo that Ken had. He suggested that they just ask the receptionist who the man was. "Baby, come on now. That's breaking confidentiality. She won't tell us that," Sheila said, with her eyebrows furrowed together. Deep down, she thought it may be at least worth the shot.

"Excuse me mam. I know this is probably a very awkward question that I'm about to ask, but do you know who that man was that the paramedics just wheeled through those doors?" Sean asked.

"I'm sorry sir, but I can't tell you that. I've got kids to feed. What concern is it of yours anyway?" the lady said, flashing Sean a flirtatious grin. Sheila stepped in front of Sean and interjected to let the receptionist know she wasn't allowing her to flirt with him right in front of her face.

"We need to know who he is because we think he's the father of my best friend who is here in labor. Supposedly he was in route here before we arrived, but I don't think he ever showed up. It's very unlike him and we're just afraid that they may have been him that they wheeled back there. Maybe he got into an accident. We're not sure, but you need to tell us whatever you know," Sheila replied directly.

The receptionist just stared back at her with a blank expression on her face. "Um, hello. Did you just hear what I said?" Sheila added. Clearly, her patience was extremely short by now. She took one step back and felt something flat, but slightly raised beneath her foot. Her blood was boiling, and she didn't have a problem going toe-to-toe with the woman at the desk.

"Come on baby, it's not worth it. I'm sure that's not him. Wait, what is that under your foot?" Sean asked.

"Wait, I just stepped on something. Look, this is a wallet," Sheila responded nervously. Sean picked up the wallet and held it in the palm of his hand.

"You think this is maybe that guy's wallet?" he asked.

"I don't know. It's worth a try to look and see," Sheila said.

Sean opened the wallet and pulled out the driver's license that was inside. He read it and then flipped it over so Sheila could see. Ken Mallory. "Shit! This can't be happening. Ok, he's going to be ok. Um, can you tell me which room Candice Mallory is in? We need to get there right away," Sheila said.

"Yeah, she's in 503. Make a right at the end of the hall and the elevator will be on your left. I'm sorry about your friend, if that's him they just took back there," the lady responded. Her countenance changed as she realized there must have been something seriously wrong going on.

"Great, thank you," Sheila said. She and Sean walked briskly through the double doors to get to Cookie's room. They looked around cautiously to see if they could see Ken along the way. They made it all the way to the elevator; he was nowhere in sight. There was one lady already inside who was going up to the third floor.

● ● ●

"Great," Sheila thought. Of course, there had to be someone else on the elevator holding them up. The elevator quickly dinged and bounced as it came to a halt on the third floor. The doors opened, and a short, petite woman quickly scurried out. As the door drew back to a close, she recognized Ken on the stretcher at a distance. They must have been getting ready to prepare him for a room.

"Is that him?" Sean said, looking at the stretcher and then back at Sheila.

"I'm pretty sure it is. That's got to be him," she said.

"Ok, then let's get off here first," Sean said. They rushed up to the stretcher. The paramedics and the nurses quickly held them back.

"Excuse me. This man has been badly injured. Please give him his space. Are you members of the family? If so, we really need to get him stabilized before he's allowed to have any visitors," said the nurse.

"Listen, we're not exactly family, but we may as well be. He's the father of my best friend's baby. She's here on the fifth floor now about to give birth. She thought he was on his way. I don't know the whole story, but I'm pretty sure she doesn't know that this happened. Her dad is up there too. We just don't know what to do at this point," Sheila sobbed. Her tough exterior was slowly crumbling.

"Oh, my goodness. What room is the mother in?" the nurse asked.

"She's in 503. We were headed up there until we saw Ken on the stretcher," Sheila said.

* * *

"Yeah, so what do we do? She's going to want to know where he is," Sean said.

"Just try to make sure she's as calm as possible. Like I said, he's pretty banged up. So, you don't want to exacerbate her stress levels right now. That won't be good for the baby," the nurse said.

"Ok, we'll try our best then. Do you know what happened to Ken?" Sheila asked, looking at him on the stretcher. He was still conscious as she could see him making subtle movements. However, his clothes were bloody and there were visible bruises on his face.

"Thank you for your help, mam," Sean said.

"Sure, he won't be ready for visitors right now but we'll find a way to get the baby to him when he or she is born. He was involved in an accident. I think that will give him an extra will to live," she said, cautiously lowering her voice.

"Wait. Will to live? Are you saying he's that badly injured?" Sheila asked.

"I'm afraid so. Again, I wouldn't alarm the mother with all this news right now. I'm a Christian woman and God has the last say. I'm just being honest with you, from a medical perspective. Please, let's keep this between us," the nurse said.

"This is so unreal, but we will get through it. I'll check in a little later when I get the chance to sneak away. Thank you again," Sheila said.

* * *

Sean and Sheila walked away and headed back to the elevator. Ken still wasn't moving much. They honestly couldn't tell if he knew they were there. Sheila exhaled deeply and threw her arms around Sean's neck when they got on the elevator.

● ● ●

Chapter 28

"I just don't know what it is with Cookie. Almost our whole friendship, that girl has never been able to catch a break. Most people wouldn't know it just by looking at her on the outside. I just thought her struggles were finally over. She can't lose him Sean. She just can't," Sheila cried. Her tears made a small pool on top of his shoulder.

As soon as the elevator opened, they turned the corner to look for Cookie's room. They would likely have to just stand outside the room, as they were sure that Bill would be inside with Cookie. Sheila and Sean arrived at the room and knocked on the door. Bill peeked out, with a look of excitement and disappointment all at once. He was expecting Ken to be standing on the other side of the door.

"Hey Sheila and Sean, you made it here pretty quickly. Good to see you. It might be a while. They're trying to see if she will need an epidural after all. Have you heard from Ken by chance?" Bill added

"Heard from Ken? No, we just came straight here," Sheila said, hoping that Bill wouldn't be able to detect her lie. However, she knew he was always a quick-witted man. She wouldn't be able to fool him for long, especially since Ken was just two floors below them in the same hospital.

"Well, as you can see, he's not here. I could strangle that boy right now. He should have beat her here. Maybe Cookie doesn't need him in her life after all," his voice trailed off.

● ● ●

"What do you mean?" Sheila asked, with a confused look on her face.

"Nothing. Nothing at all. I'm just frustrated. If you want to take my place for a while I can stay out here and keep Sean company for a bit," he replied.

"Ok, that sounds good. Wait. I can't stand here and just lie to your face like this," Sheila uttered.

"Daddy, please don't leave," Cookie said from inside the room. She could see him standing outside the room, through the crack in the door. Although she was in a great deal of pain, she was fully aware that Ken still hadn't arrived. She needed her husband there with her. Bill was the next best thing and he was doing a phenomenal job supporting her.

"I'm not going anywhere baby. I'm right here. I'll be right back in, I promise," Bill reassured her.

Sheila looked at Sean and then back at Bill with a blank expression on her face. Bill could see she was fighting back tears and Sean even showed a sour emotional expression on his face. "I'm so sorry," she whispered.

"You better start talking fast. What is all this about? Do you know something my baby doesn't know about Ken?" he asked.

"It's not that. We think Ken was in an accident on the way here. We got here at the same time as the paramedics were wheeling him to a room on the third floor. He's banged up bad and he can't have any visitors right now. The nurse said after the delivery, they want to try to bring the baby in there. They think it will give him

* * *

something to look forward to," she answered, wiping the tears that were beginning to flow down her cheeks.

"No. This can't be. That girl has had more than her fair share of heartache. She doesn't need this now too," Bill said.

"I know, we're praying he makes a speedy recovery. The doctors and the nurse are being very attentive to him. I'm sure he will pull right through this," Sheila responded.

"Yeah, God will pull him through. I know he will. She didn't mean to do what she did to him. Their story won't end like this," Bill said.

"What exactly do you mean?" Sean asked.

"Oh, nothing. It's too long of a story to go into now. I'll have to fill you in later or better yet, I should probably let Cookie do that. Sheila, I'm sure she'll be happy to see you. Do you mind going in with her for a little while? I'm famished and starting to feel light-headed. I'm just going to get a bit to eat and come right back. Sean, do you want to join me?"

"Sure. Will you be alright, baby?" Sean asked.

"I'll be fine. Go on and get some bonding time in with Bill. He won't bite. Besides, they only let one person in at a time," she smiled.

Sheila walked into the room and the doctors were directing Cookie to keep pushing. "Sheila, my friend! Thank you for coming to see me. You are my sister. I love you," Cookie said.

* * *

236

"I love you too. Of course, I wouldn't miss this for the world. Plus, I have to prove a point that you're having a girl, like I said," she laughed. Sheila grabbed Cookie's hand and immediately realized it was a mistake. Cookie squeezed her hands so hard that it felt like she was crushing her bones.

"Ice. I need some ice. Can you help me?" Cookie pleaded.

"Stay right there. I'll get it for her," the nurse exclaimed. She quickly scurried out of the room to get the ice for Cookie.

"Sheila. I don't think he loves me anymore. He didn't even show up. How could he not show up to see his child being born? How could he do this?" Cookie asked as her face twisted in agony.

"Cookie, we need you to focus for a moment. Please stop pushing. The baby is coming, but the umbilical cord is wrapped around its neck. We're going to have to twist the baby around. Just please don't push anymore right now. We don't want to harm the baby," Dr. Tinton said.

"Come on Cookie. You can do this. Just please be still. It's almost over. She's almost here," Sheila said.

"Don't make me laugh. You are such a nut, but I love you," Cookie said, as she started crying uncontrollably.

"Ok, I'll be good. Cookie? Ken loves you with all his heart. It may seem strange, but he has a good reason for not being here right now. I know he does. He loves you and he'll be here right on time, when it counts," Sheila assured Cookie and rubbed her shoulder.

"Cookie! Cookie! We need you to be very still right now. I'm going to reach inside and turn the baby around. It's going to be ok, but you have to do as I say," Dr. Tinton urged. He shot Sheila a concerned glance. She knew from his facial expression that this was serious.

The room was completely silent. Sheila wiped away the tears that were streaming down Cookie's face to her ears. She stroked her hair back and laughed to herself. Cookie was so meticulous about her appearance and she usually would have been very concerned about her hair still being intact. However, it didn't matter right now. She still looked as beautiful as ever. She had a glow around her that filled the room.

"Sheila, is anything going to happen to my baby?" Cookie asked in a frightful, almost childlike tone.

"No, sweetheart. The baby is going to be just fine. She's either going to be a dancer or an athlete. That's my prediction. I mean, how else would she get the umbilical cord wrapped around her neck? The baby was just moving faster than the world was ready for. That's all," Sheila smiled.

"Yeah, you know you are probably right, especially with the way this baby was kicking in the last few days," Cookie replied, trying to forge a smile, through the pain, on her face.

Meanwhile, Bill and Sean were walking back towards Cookie's room. "Well, this is what you have to look forward to man. This is the most beautiful day of any man's life. I just wish Ken was here to see it. I knew something had to be wrong. He's made his share of faults, like we all have, but I know he would love to be here to see his child being born," Bill said.

* * *

"I'm actually readier for kids than Sheila is. I think she's a little more cautious and wants to make sure we have everything in place first. Yeah, I don't know Ken all that well. But, I do know he would want to be in that room right now. He loves Cookie something terrible," he said.

"He does. I can tell. All men mess up from time to time. I did too in my marriage with Lisa. That's just human nature," Bill said.

"There's no hope then," Sean laughed.

"Watch out now, youngster. I'm just telling the truth. I like to deal with reality. Nobody's perfect," Bill said.

"I hear you. We are all a work in progress. Hey, how about we go down to the room where Ken is to check on him?" Sean suggested.

"Yes, that's a great idea. I really hope he's ok. Let's check him out. He's a strong man. I know he'll pull through this. He has to. He has a family to be here for now," Bill replied. He sounded more like he was trying to convince himself more than Sean.

Sean and Bill made their way down to the third floor. The nurse on duty immediately recognized Sean and walked over towards him and Bill. "Hey, he's resting now but this actually may be a good time to see him because we will be in and out running different tests," she said.

"Ok, I'm sorry I didn't get your name when we were up here earlier. I'm Sean. I guess we were so distracted by Ken's condition earlier that we didn't get a chance to introduce ourselves. This is my wife's friend's father, Bill. His daughter is the one that's having the baby," Sean said.

"Well, hello there. My name is Monica. So nice to officially meet you Sean and nice to meet you too, Bill," Monica smiled at them.

"Nice meeting you too, Monica. Yes, I will soon be Grandpa Bill," Bill gleamed.

"I know you've got to be so excited. I do have a bit of an update about Ken's condition. He probably isn't feeling well enough for visitors right now, but I think he will be coherent to at least know who you are. He has a few broken ribs and um, a fracture in his skull, directly above the right temple.

"But he's going to be ok, right? Bill asked in a hopeful tone.

"It's really too early to say right now, but we are definitely hopeful, as he is pretty bruised up. I just want to warn you of that before I take you in to see him," Monica said.

"Ok, well I guess now is as good a time as any to see him," Sean said. He could see the fear in Bill's eyes. Monica tried her best to be positive and diplomatic, but Ken's condition was not hopeful.

They slowly walked into the room, as not to disturb Ken. Although Sean caught a glimpse of him earlier, he didn't get a chance to see his face well. Now, he and Bill were witnessing the aftermath of Ken's accident, up close and personal. Ken groaned when they walked through the door and he tried to lift his hand. However, it appeared as if he was unable to raise it too high.

"Hey there, Ken. I don't know if you can hear me, but you have to pull through this. You can't leave that baby without her father. She may not admit it right now, but Cookie needs you and she forgives you," Bill said.

● ● ●

Ken let out a faint grunt as if to say, "Thank you" for Bill's affirmation. Sean stood there in awe, looking at Ken's face. There were several bruises, including the most noticeable one on the right side of his head where Monica said the fracture was. Although there was a large piece of gauze covering part of his face, Sean could see that the right side of his head had already begun to swell.

"Yeah man, I need you to experience all the tips and tricks of being a father first so you can pass them down to me," Sean chimed in.

Another nurse quickly came in to draw some blood from Ken. She tested his reflexes, but he was mostly unresponsive.

Bill looked on with his arms folded and tapped his foot. He was always a cool and collected man, but his nerves were starting to get the best of him.

"Bill and Sean, I'm afraid we'll have to ask you to step out now. I'm so sorry. I'll find you and keep you posted if there are any changes in his status," she said.

"Please do. Ok, I guess we will get out of your hair for now then. Thanks Monica," Sean said.

"Yes, thanks for everything Monica. I'm glad I at least got a chance to see him," Bill added solemnly.

Several hours had passed and Bill was starting to feel drained, even after eating earlier. He was naturally a night owl, but all the stress from the day zapped his energy. "Hey Sean, what do you think about Ken? How did he look to you?" Bill asked.

Sean paused for a moment to collect his thoughts. He wanted to be positive, but there was no denying that Ken was very seriously hurt. His injuries would surely take some time to heal from. "You know, I think it will take him some time but I think he'll be healed pretty quickly to make a strong, upstanding father. How about you?"

Sometimes you must lie to dull the sting of the truth. Sean and Bill both knew that Ken's condition was not looking good. He just didn't have the heart to tell Bill the cold, hard truth that they both already knew. There was no way Ken was going to bounce back from this.

• • •

Two Years Later

It was an unusually cold Saturday morning. Alicia sipped on a mocha latte at Starbucks, while she waited for Cookie to arrive. The steam from the coffee danced across her face to give her comfort from the cool temperature. For a moment, the steam also cooled her anxious nerves as she wondered what Cookie wanted to meet with her about.

Sheila called Cookie just as she was parking her car to meet Alicia. "Hey girl, is everything ok? I hope Breanna is not giving you any problems. She's in this phase now where she likes to climb on everything," Cookie explained.

"Hey, it's not that. Cookie, did you know there was a small bottled of opened vodka on the side of her bag?" Sheila asked cautiously.

"Oh, my God. Sheila. I'm so sorry. I'm really embarrassed. Did she get inside the bottle?" Cookie asked. Her heart dropped to the pit of her stomach and she was mortified that she could be so careless.

"No, luckily I grabbed it from her before she could screw the top off. Please be careful with her Cookie. Please," Sheila responded, as her voice cracked on the other line. She didn't want to add insult to injury, but this was the third time a similar instance had happened with Breanna within the last two months.

"I will. That's why I'm going to get help. I promise, I'm going to get better. I'm here to meet Alicia now, but thank you so much. I'll make it up to you. I love you," Cookie said.

* * *

"No need to make up anything. We're sisters, remember?" Sheila said, wiping the tears from her eyes.

"Yes, my sister. I love you. I'll call you back," Cookie replied. She let out a deep sigh before she opened the door to get out of the car.

Alicia took another sip of the coffee and looked up to see Cookie walking briskly through the door. She looked casually stunning, without being overdone. The only thing that looked out of character was her eyes. Her eyes looked lifeless and dark, almost as if she was under the influence of drugs.

"Hello, Alicia. How are you? Thank you for meeting me today," Cookie said.

"Sure, of course. Look, Cookie I know we haven't seen each other since the funeral. I just want to apologize again for keeping such a big secret like that from you. I swear, Ken and I never did anything outside of that one night. I didn't know about you back then. I just couldn't tell you because of Charles. I hope you understand and have found some way to forgive me," Alicia said.

"Oh, yes. I have forgiven you. I forgave Ken eventually too. It was just too late at that point," Cookie said, as her voice trailed off.

"I promise, if there was a way I could make up for any pain I've caused you, I would," Alicia replied, tears welling up in her eyes.

"Is that so? That's what I wanted to meet with you about today. I have to go away for a little while. I won't be able to take care of Breanna in the way that she deserves during that time. My father is getting older and I don't have any family members I can depend on. So, I would like to know if you and Charles could take Breanna for me. I'm not sure how long it will be, maybe six months or a little longer. She needs a stable home. She deserves that. I'm not my best self-right now to give her what she needs," Cookie said, shifting her eyes away from Alicia, as she tried not to cry.

"Wow, I'm speechless. I'm truly honored that you trust me enough to look after your daughter. That's a big undertaking though. I would have to talk to Charles about it first. What's wrong? Where are you going?" Alicia inquired.

"I have to face my fears like a big girl, finally. I'm not mentally stable enough to be the mother Breana needs right now. It's not fair to her. I just need to recharge for a bit. I'm going to rehab and then everything will be fine again. That's what I keep telling myself at least. Please, if you don't do it for me, please do it for her," Cookie pleaded.

"Ok, I understand your plight as a mother. I'll see if I can work my magic with Charles. I don't have much pull with him these days, but I will try my best," Alicia said.

"Thanks so much for thinking about it. How is Lance doing? Is he still feeling great?" Cookie asked.

"Yes, thanks for asking. He's back to normal as if nothing ever happened. He's doing really well," Alicia replied, fighting back her tears. Every time she looked at Lance, she was reminded of her secret and how it ultimately came to light. Nonetheless, she would do it all over again the same way, if It meant that Ken would still be the vessel to save his life.

• • •

"That's really nice to hear. I'm happy about that. Alicia, how did you and Charles move past everything once the secret was out about Lance?" Cookie asked.

"How did we? It's not all in the past. It's still an ongoing process. The only thing I can really do is take it day by day. He has his angry moments and I just let him get it out. He deserves that much at least. I'm really grateful it didn't turn out nastier than it did," she said, feeling selfish after she uttered those words out loud.

"I can imagine. Well, I didn't want to hold you long, but please think about what I said," Cookie said.

"I will definitely let you know Cookie," Alicia said.

"Ok, great. Please send Charles and Lance my love," Cookie responded.

"I will do that for sure. It was nice seeing you Cookie. You take care," Alicia said.

"Thank you. It was really nice seeing you too," Cookie replied. She hugged Alicia and they both parted ways to go back to their respective vehicles.

Cookie drove in silence all the way home. Her tears blurred her vision through an already gloomy, cloudy day. She hated the thought of giving away her daughter to the woman that made a baby with Ken years ago. She hated the thought of giving up Breanna period. However, it was her only choice. Her father couldn't take her and Sheila was soon expecting her own first child with Sean. That would be unfair to impose on her friend like that, no matter how much she insisted otherwise.

● ● ●

For two years straight, she kept telling herself that Ken's death happened because of the car accident. However, the weight of her lies had finally started to unravel her mental state. That's when the drinking started. He would still be alive today if she hadn't exploded in a fit of rage the day she went into the closet to get her gun and kill him dead. She should have listened to him and calmed her temper. Charles forgave Alicia. Why couldn't she have done the same thing with Ken?

Cookie decided to stop in Whole Foods to pick up some ingredients to make dinner. She wanted to come over and cook for Sheila to show her appreciation for watching Breanna. Cookie had a craving for some stuffed bell peppers. She needed some ground turkey, bell peppers, red potatoes and tomato sauce to go along with the items she already had at home. That was one of Ken's favorite meals. She missed him every day, but today she was stronger than usual. At least the meal would make her feel closer to him.

As soon as she walked in the store, Cookie was already frustrated with herself that she didn't follow her first mind and go into the Whole Foods that was closer to home. The layout of the store was different than the one she visited frequently. Cookie felt like someone was behind her when she was in the meat section getting the ground turkey. She turned around, pleasantly surprised to see that it was Mike. He didn't seem to recognize her at first, until they made eye contact. There was no turning back now.

"Cookie? Look at you! How have you been? It's been a while. Where is the little one? I know she has got to be spoiled rotten. She's so beautiful," Mike said, with a fire and excitement in his eyes. His entire countenance changed once he realized it was Cookie.

"Mike! Oh, it's so good to see you too. Breanna is good, telling me and everyone else what to do," she laughed. She squeezed Mike hard and hugged him a little longer than he expected. He welcomed it, although it caught him off guard. Cookie had been very standoffish with him recently. Truthfully, she was ashamed and didn't know how to face him now.

"Well, um, you look great as usual," he said, trying to lighten the awkwardness.

"Thank you. So do you. How are you doing after the divorce?" Cookie asked.

"Oh, it's great. I mean, everything is finalized so I'm great. Single and free. We have been divorced for about a year now. It's hard getting back out in this dating scene, but I'm making it," he said.

"Ah, a handsome man like you will find the perfect woman in no time. I'm sure of it," Cookie said.

"I appreciate the kind vote of confidence. How about we grab a bite to eat sometime soon or maybe just some coffee?" he figured now was as perfect time as any to shoot his shot. Cookie seemed to be more receptive to him now than she had been in recent years. Although he was sad about Ken's tragic death, he didn't want to miss an open opportunity.

"I would love to. How about this Wednesday evening? I have to be transparent with you. I'm getting prepared to go away for a while. Hopefully it will only be for a few months. I need to get some help to mentally reset everything from the last couple years," Cookie said, with a cracked voice and watery eyes.

"Ok, sure. Wednesday is perfect. I'm sorry if that was too forward. We don't have to do it if it makes you uncomfortable. Where are you going?"

"Oh, a woman can't divulge all of her secrets. I will tell you it's a much-needed time to unplug and really get back to my old self. When I come back, I'll be revitalized and back to my old self but better," Cookie replied.

"Ok, well that sounds good. Just keep me posted. I'll be here waiting on you. Is 7:00 pm on Wednesday good? You are still a mysterious woman, I see," Mike said, with a pleasant but disappointed look on his face.

"Hmmmm, yes 7:00 pm is perfect. Mysterious? Do you think you will ever solve me Mike?" Cookie smiled.

* * *

An excerpt from *A Swipe in the Wrong Direction*; a novella coming in 2020.

"Ugh, goodness," Lenny groaned as the sunlight started to peer through the curtain. He tried to sit up in the bed, but his head felt too heavy. He looked over at the clock. 8:03 am. He assumed he had only been asleep a couple of hours or so. He scanned the room for his phone and in the process, saw the mess that had been made.

There was an opened condom wrapper near his head on the pillow. Two empty bottles of champagne were on the nightstand, with his underwear hanging off the corner. His pants and shirt were off. But his undershirt was still on. There was a faint scent of some type of vanilla and berry scented fragrance on his upper lip. All the remnants of last night's escapades were strewn across the room.

Boom! Boom! Boom!

His head was spinning again. He had to be dreaming. Lenny could hear voices on the other side of the door yelling, "Open up! Rise and shine!" He looked over at the clock again. 9:54 am. Great. He was hoping it was closer to noon. Lenny forced himself out of bed, threw some shorts on and answered the door.

"Aren't you guys supposed to be still sleeping? We didn't even get back here until almost 4:00 am last night," Lenny complained.

"So what? It's your birthday celebration. Suck it up. You're going to continue to have a good time for the next couple of days that we're here and there's nothing you can do about it. But, you're on your own tab as of today," Ben laughed.

* * *